W.i.t.c.h.

Will   Irma   Taranee   Cornelia   Hay Lin

A Bridge Between Worlds

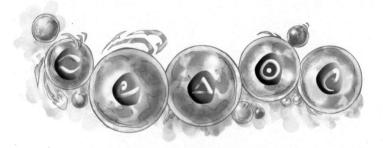

Adapted by ELIZABETH LENHARD

VOLO

an imprint of
HYPERION BOOKS FOR CHILDREN
New York

If you purchased this book without a cover, you should be aware that this book is stolen property. It was reported as "unsold and destroyed" to the publisher, and neither the author nor the publisher has received any payment for this "stripped" book.

© 2004 Disney Enterprises, Inc.

W.I.T.C.H. Will Irma Taranee Cornelia Hay Lin is a trademark of Disney Enterprises, Inc.
Volo® is a registered trademark of Disney Enterprises, Inc.
Volo/Hyperion Books for Children are imprints of Disney Children's Group, L.L.C.

All rights reserved. No part of this book may be reproduced or transmitted in any form or by any means, electronic or mechanical, including photocopying, recording, or by any information storage and retrieval system, without written permission from the publisher. For information address Volo Books, 114 Fifth Avenue, New York, New York 10011-5690.

Printed in the United States of America
First Edition
1 3 5 7 9 10 8 6 4 2

This book is set in 12/16.5 Hiroshige Book.
ISBN 0-7868-5138-4
Visit www.clubwitch.com

ELYON'S HOUSE, ON THE OUTSKIRTS OF HEATHERFIELD...

THE ELECTRICITY'S OUT. MAYBE WE'D BETTER POSTPONE THE INSPECTION.

I DON'T THINK SO. IT'S NOT EVERY DAY AN ENTIRE FAMILY DISAPPEARS INTO THIN AIR!

WHAT DO WE HAVE HERE?

ELYON

DRAWINGS BY ELYON BROWN, FROM WHEN SHE WAS SIX UNTIL RIGHT BEFORE HER DISAPPEARANCE. INTERESTING!

HMMM. THERE'S A RECURRING IMAGE. IT LOOKS LIKE A MAGICAL CITY.

LOOK! THIS ONE IS COMPLETE. THE CITY, AGAIN. AND ABOVE IT. . .

. . . A GIRL WEARING A CROWN. FLYING AROUND AND SHINING LIKE THE SUN.

LOOKS LIKE DROPS OF WATER FELL RIGHT ON HER FACE. THE COLORS ARE ALL SMEARED. TOO BAD.

OH, ELYON! WHERE ARE YOU? WHAT HAPPENED TO YOU?

MAY I COME IN?

KNOCK KNOCK

ONE

Hay Lin had magical powers. She was a Guardian of the Veil. She could fly. She could transform herself into an all-powerful being. She had even fought against evil guards at a palace in another world! But there was one thing that Hay Lin couldn't get out of—cleaning up her family's restaurant after a big party.

Her parents were very strict about having her help out at their restaurant, the Silver Dragon. After a huge party in the banquet room, the back area was a total disaster. The night before, people had filled the place, having a great time, eating lots of food, and making a mess.

While other people she knew napped or snacked their way through the weekend, Hay

Lin did the cleanup thing, scrubbing, sweeping, and polishing.

Normally, Hay Lin didn't care. She liked helping her parents out and took pride in her family's restaurant. Today, however, she didn't have time to stay and help. She had to get out of cleanup duty, so that she could join her fellow Guardians in plotting their latest mission.

Irma had called her early, saying that everyone would be meeting at her house to discuss what to do about Elyon. Elyon was Cornelia's best friend and had been missing from Heatherfield for a long time. Hay Lin and her friends knew exactly where Elyon was, but it wasn't as if they could tell the Heatherfield police that Elyon had been taken to another world called Metamoor by a snake-man creature named Cedric! Helping Elyon was up to the Guardians of the Veil.

Hay Lin peered into the banquet room. She saw Cornelia and Taranee talking to her dad and doing their best to get her out of cleanup duty. When they had showed up a few minutes before to pick her up, she had had to explain to them that there was no way her dad was going to let her go out.

Cornelia thought that she would try talking to Hay Lin's dad. "Will you let Hay Lin go out with us?" Cornelia asked him. "Pleeeeease?" She raised her slender arms from beneath her fringed brown poncho and clasped her hands together, pleading.

Hay Lin's father was so busy sweeping he didn't even look up as he answered her. "I'm sorry, Cornelia," he said. "But Hay Lin *has* to help me clean up the restaurant."

"Irma's waiting for us!" Cornelia protested.

Exactly, Hay Lin wailed inwardly. I can't stay home while Cornelia, Taranee, and Will all go to Irma's house. Irma is one of my best friends *and* a fellow Guardian. All of us need to be together to come up with a perfect plan.

Being a Guardian, Hay Lin thought with a little shiver—it's both the best and worst thing that's ever happened to me. In any case, it's definitely the craziest!

As Cornelia continued to coax Hay Lin's dad into letting Hay Lin go out, Hay Lin leaned against the wall. She couldn't help grinning as she remembered the day the whole adventure had begun, right upstairs in her apartment.

Hay Lin, Will, Irma, Taranee, and Cornelia

had all gathered in the kitchen to discuss a very freaky phenomenon: they'd all been having the same dream! Or at least, they'd been dreaming about the same object—a glass orb cradled in an ornate and unusual silver clasp. When Hay Lin sketched the amulet from her own dream, every one of her friends had recognized it. But none of them had had any idea what it meant.

As they'd pondered that group vision, Irma had crunched on a big handful of the almond cookies she'd grabbed.

That was *not* unusual, Hay Lin thought with a smile. Irma's got a big craving for sweets and an even bigger appetite for adventure.

Taranee and Will, who had both just moved to Heatherfield, were more reserved. They'd simply leaned their elbows on the big table, looking pensive and troubled. Cornelia, meanwhile, had been her usual stubborn, rational self. She'd refused to believe that the dream could be anything more than mere coincidence.

That is, Hay Lin recalled with another grin, until my grandmother walked into the kitchen and proved Cornelia wrong. She'd pulled out of her pocket the very amulet we'd all been dreaming about—the Heart of Candracar.

Even after Hay Lin's grandmother had explained what Candracar was, the place had remained mysterious. All the girls knew was that Candracar was a beautiful place in the middle of infinity—a place that could only be reached by crossing an air-colored bridge.

It was the home of wise, benevolent beings, the wisest of whom was the Oracle. He saw all, knew all, and worked to protect the earth from evil.

The girls had quickly come into contact with one of the evil forces who had concerned the Oracle. He was the ruthless young ruler of a distant world called Metamoor. Under his reign, Metamoor was forced to remain dark and Gothic. Oppressing his own citizens wasn't enough for Prince Phobos—he wanted to control the earth as well.

The Oracle wasn't about to let *that* happen. To protect the earth, he'd created the Veil. The Veil was an invisible but impassable barrier between good and evil.

This system had worked quite nicely for a long time. Now, though, the Veil was full of holes—literally! The dawn of the new millennium had caused twelve tears to open up in the barrier. In turn, those tears had created passageways between Metamoor and the earth. All twelve of those portals led straight to Heatherfield.

Hay Lin smiled as she thought of the great responsibility she and her friends had been given.

Will, Irma, Taranee, Cornelia, and I are the Guardians of the Veil, Hay Lin thought. We have to keep Metamoorians away from Heatherfield and close every portal we find. And we have to keep our identities secret!

The five friends all had magical powers. Will was the Keeper of the Heart of Candracar. The crystal orb, brimming with power, lay inside her body. When the Guardians were in trouble, the orb was released from Will's palm. Its pulsing energy whisked away the girls' ordinary clothes and replaced them with funky, striped leggings, playful purple miniskirts, and midriff-baring tops. The Guardians' bodies changed, too. They grew taller, curvier, and more beautiful. They even sprouted wings!

Of course, I am the only one who can actually fly, Hay Lin thought with a smile.

With their changes in appearance, four of the Guardians also acquired the powers of the earth's four elements.

Cornelia, grounded and sensible, was all about the earth. She could make plants grow and dirt move. She could even make tree leaves reconfigure themselves into a picture of her crush.

Taranee, meanwhile, could hold fire in the palm of her hand, and Irma wielded power over water.

And me? Hay Lin thought now, with a happy little hop. I'm the breezy one, with power over the air. If you ask me, it's definitely the best magical mojo to have.

Yes, but it is not meant for fun, little Hay Lin.

Hay Lin came crashing out of her daydream as a voice in the back of her mind chided her. Despite the admonishing tone, the thin, reedy voice was sweet and affectionate. It belonged to Hay Lin's grandmother, who had died soon after telling the Guardians about their magical powers. Although she was gone, Hay Lin still felt her presence.

I know my magic is not just for fun and games, Hay Lin thought as she continued to hide in the hallway. Grandma was once a Guardian of the Veil, too. We're totally cut from the same cloth—even if her Guardian getup was probably a little different from ours. And of course, she's right about my magic: it's no toy. It's way too powerful to be just a toy.

Hay Lin and her friends were getting used to their powers. Both in Heatherfield and in Metamoor's mazelike capital city, Meridian, the girls had butted heads with Cedric, a slimy snake who sometimes disguised himself as a long-haired young man. Cedric served Phobos, tirelessly acting out the prince's evil and deceit. He'd tried to do away with the Guardians many times. Recently, he'd even tried to harm Will, only minutes after she'd saved *his* life. With that dishonorable act, he'd lost the loyalty of his henchman, a big blue ox of a monster named Vathek. Now, Vathek was part of Metamoor's team of rebels, who, like the Guardians, wanted to oust Phobos from his throne.

It's pretty hard to believe Elyon used to be just another kid at the Sheffield Institute, Hay Lin thought.

That had all changed when Cedric—in his human disguise—had lured Elyon to a bookshop one night. Instead of taking her on the date she'd expected, he'd told Elyon that she was a princess of Metamoor, stolen from her royal family by traitors who had brought her to Heatherfield and posed as her real parents.

That wasn't the whole truth, Hay Lin thought with a scowl, Cedric had told Elyon that her adoptive parents had kidnapped her to keep her from ascending to the throne. But actually, they had set out to save her from her power-hungry brother—Phobos, who had wanted the throne for himself!

Elyon's adoptive parents and nursemaid had intervened. The green-skinned, lizardlike couple and the red-eyed, rough-skinned nanny had spirited the baby through a portal in the Veil and brought her to Heatherfield.

In Heatherfield, the couple had been transformed into humans—Thomas and Eleanor Brown. The nurse had taken on the shape of Mrs. Rudolph, a math teacher at Sheffield Institute, where the girls went to school. The Browns and Mrs. Rudolph intended to keep Elyon safe from her brother's clutches until she was old enough to assume the throne as the Light of Meridian.

It had been a perfect plan—until Cedric got to Elyon. After that, Elyon had moved to her brother's cold castle in Metamoor and disappeared from Heatherfield. Her parents had disappeared, too.

And nobody, Hay Lin thought with wide eyes, knows what's happened to them! All my friends and I *do* know is, Elyon became our enemy that day. She helped kidnap Taranee and tried to convince her that nobody even missed her. She attacked us with lots of stunning and superpowerful magic.

The only thing she didn't have, Hay Lin thought with a grateful shiver, was a group of friends at her side. But *we* did! That's why Elyon lost every battle she fought with us.

Now, it looked as though Elyon herself realized she'd been deceived. She was questioning Cedric's story and reaching out in small ways to the Guardians. But Hay Lin and her friends still didn't know if they could truly trust her.

Hay Lin returned her attention to Cornelia's ongoing conversation with her dad. She had to get to Irma's house to make a plan of action. Cornelia was trying to help, but her negotiations were *not* going well.

"The party was crazier than ever last night," Hay Lin's dad was saying stubbornly. "Without Hay Lin's help, I'll never have the restaurant back in shape in time for the regular dinner crowd."

Taranee turned away from Cornelia and Hay Lin's father and scuttled over to Hay Lin. "What a mess!" Taranee whispered to Hay Lin. "What should we do?"

Hay Lin gazed out at the banquet room's scuffed tile floor, smashed cups, and discarded party hats. She found herself fantasizing about a great west wind, swooping in through one of the Silver Dragon's big, round windows to scoop up all that trash and carry it away.

If only, she thought with a sigh, something as crazy as that could actually hap—

Suddenly, Hay Lin gasped.

Wait a minute, she thought. I keep forgetting. When you're magic, anything *can* happen.

Well, just about anything. Hay Lin might have powers over the wind, air, and sky, but she still couldn't control her father. For that mega-task, she'd need her friends.

"Distract my dad," Hay Lin mouthed to Cornelia from the doorway. Cornelia cocked her head to one side. She'd clearly understood Hay Lin's message.

"I'll take care of the rest," Hay Lin assured her friends.

Cornelia straightened her head and took a step closer to Hay Lin's father.

"Hay Lin says you're some kind of ornithologist," she piped up. "Is that true?"

"Huh?" Hay Lin's dad said. He looked up excitedly from his sweeping. "Well," he replied, his thin cheeks flushing with pride, "I'm not exactly an expert in birds, but I do know a thing or two."

"It's just that I saw an interesting bird on my way in to the restaurant," Cornelia said. She winked over her shoulder at Hay Lin in her hiding place. "I was wondering what it was. Maybe you could come look out the front window with me and tell me if you think it's a crow?"

Hay Lin slapped a hand over her mouth to keep from laughing out loud.

Cornelia's brilliant, she thought. There's no way my dad can resist the caw of a crow!

Sure enough, when Cornelia marched confidently through the swinging door that separated the banquet room from the dining room in the front of the restaurant, Dad ditched his broom and eagerly followed her.

The moment Cornelia and her father disappeared through the doorway, Hay Lin popped into the room.

"Step aside, Taranee," she said breathlessly. As Taranee flattened herself against the wall, Hay Lin looked around the disheveled banquet room.

"I'll just say this with a bit of flair," she declared as she threw her arms over her head. "Obey me now, powers of air!"

Hay Lin felt her stomach lurch as jolts of magic immediately began to course through her. The energy swam through her veins, shimmied around the chambers of her heart, and finally zinged up her arms until it crackled out through her fingertips. The magic burst from her hands, shooting into the banquet room in the form of dramatic silver rays.

In the middle of the room, the swirls of magic converged and began spinning like a top.

They gathered speed.

They expanded outward.

And they started making *quite* a racket.

Whooooooooosssshhh!

Hay Lin's magic had become a small tornado whirling across the scuffed Silver Dragon floor. Napkins, paper plates, and paper cups were all sucked into the vortex of air without a fight.

Hay Lin's hands tingled as she moved the tornado around the room, using a combination of finger wiggles, directive thoughts, and old-fashioned gut instinct. Everything the tornado touched—save the tables and chairs—was mercilessly scooped up. The whirlwind left the floors and tabletops gleaming in its wake.

Wow! Hay Lin thought gleefully. All these years, I've been working my tail off to help my parents keep the Silver Dragon sparkling. Now, my magic does the heavy lifting for me!

The knowledge made Hay Lin want to hop around the room with joy. If only she'd had the time. Instead, she had to finish her job *and* keep tabs on her father. Through the crack between the swinging doors, Hay Lin could just make him out, talking to Cornelia as he looked out the window.

"That bird up there, under that ledge?" her dad was saying. "It looks more like a jackdaw."

"A what?" Cornelia answered loudly, glancing over her shoulder at the banquet room doors. "How is that different from a crow?"

Hay Lin suppressed another giggle. Cornelia was playing dumb, which was as ludicrous as . . . well, as ludicrous as me trying to save the world, Hay Lin thought with a shrug. Put that way, I guess *nothing* seems so unbelievable anymore.

Hay Lin focused hard and channeled all her magical energy into the minitornado. The cyclone was jammed with trash by now. Just before it all overflowed, Hay Lin was able to guide it to a garbage bag in the corner.

Crackle-tinkle-crash!

The tornado tossed its load neatly into the plastic bag.

Whoooosh!

Now the funnel was whirling itself away. Within seconds, it had died down to a gentle breeze.

"Well, thanks for the explanation, sir!" Cornelia said.

Hay Lin looked up. Through the porthole windows of the swinging doors, she could see Cornelia and her father approaching the banquet room. Cornelia was practically shrieking her thanks to Hay Lin's father, so that Hay Lin would know they were coming back.

"And thank *you*, for the oh-so-subtle warning, Cornelia," Hay Lin whispered with a little laugh.

"I understood almost all of that bird lesson," Cornelia was saying now, as she and Hay Lin's father walked through the swinging doors. He was looking down at her with a pleased grin on his face.

"Don't mention it, Cornelia," he said, with pride in his voice. "All you have to do is observe the plumage and . . ."

His voice trailed off as he noticed the state of the room. Hay Lin's dad turned his back on Cornelia and gaped at the spotless, totally garbage-free banquet room!

"What happened?" he gasped.

He stared at the shining floor, the neatly draped pink tablecloths, the brimming garbage bag in the corner. Then he looked, flabbergasted, at his daughter.

Hay Lin returned his look with a sweet smile. "Now can I go out, Dad?"

"Y—yes," he stuttered, gazing again at the pristine room. "But how . . . how . . . how long did it take you to . . ."

Hay Lin felt a little flip-flop in her stomach. How on earth do I answer that one?

Luckily, Cornelia jumped to her rescue.

"Your explanation must have taken a little longer than we thought," Cornelia said quickly to Hay Lin's father. "But it was interesting! So, see you later!"

Hay Lin gave Cornelia a thumbs-up and skipped over to her flummoxed father.

"Bye, Dad!" she said. "Remind Mom that I'm having dinner at Irma's tonight!"

Dad nodded vaguely. He was still staring in bewilderment at the room. As Hay Lin slipped out the door behind her two friends, she shook her head sympathetically.

Welcome to my world, Dad, she thought. Unexplainable phenomena, magical powers, special secrets—it's all in a day's work!

TWO

As she hurried toward the front door of the Silver Dragon with Taranee and Hay Lin at her heels, Cornelia felt a surge of pride. Using cleverness to get herself out of a tight spot was always satisfying, but working her deceptive magic on a *parent* was a true accomplishment!

In this case, Cornelia admitted to herself reluctantly, Hay Lin was the one who provided the real magic. If we hadn't worked together, we'd never have pulled that little scheme off.

Cornelia cringed at the realization. As much as she loved her friends, the Guardians' whole working-as-a-team thing didn't always suit her personality. Cornelia was cool, aloof, and totally indie. When it came to after-school activities, she shunned the soccer team in favor of figure skating, the most solitary sport around. And until her bratty baby sister, Lilian, had come on to the scene, Cornelia had been an only child.

I'm just used to doing things on my own, Cornelia thought as she pushed open the door. Now that I'm part of the Power of Five, those days are over.

Cornelia sighed as she stepped outside. The skies were dark, and rain was coming down in torrents.

"This rain is so gross!" Hay Lin said, echoing Cornelia's thoughts, as she, too, stepped through the door to cower under the Silver Dragon's eaves. "I wish Irma were here to use her power over water."

See? Cornelia thought. I'm *right here* and Hay Lin just wants another Guardian. I may not have Irma's water-controlling magic, but I have something just as good in my very hand.

Cornelia thrust her secret weapon—a colorful umbrella—toward her friends and said defiantly, "Let it rain. No need to cry. My umbrella will keep us dry."

Cornelia smiled triumphantly—until she saw Hay Lin and Taranee both roll their eyes.

Then Taranee slipped out from under the eaves and dashed across the street to take cover in a phone booth while she used her cell phone.

Hay Lin piped up, "No offense, Cornelia, but even Irma's better with rhymes than that."

"What's going on?" Cornelia snapped. "Are you new members of the Irma fan club or something?"

Before Hay Lin could answer, Taranee slipped her cell phone back into her bag and darted back to her friends.

"Problem solved," she announced. Her hat's woolly earflaps bobbed against her round cheeks as she pointed down the street. "All it took was a phone call to find a way to avoid all this rain."

Cornelia followed Taranee's gaze. A car was rounding the corner and slogging up the almost-deserted block. As the navy-blue station wagon slowed down in front of the restaurant, Cornelia noted that the front bumper was plastered with stickers that said *Save the Sea Cows; Karmilla Rocks;* and *Dude, Where's My Burger?* It was unmistakably the ride of a teenage boy.

The car screeched to a halt at the curb, right in front of the three girls. As the driver's-side window lowered, Cornelia gasped. The boy behind the wheel had an oh-so-cute face and a topknot of bouncy, brown dreadlocks.

Oh, *no*! Cornelia thought. It's Taranee's brother, Peter!

Peter thrust his lanky arm out into the rain to wave at the Guardians. He had a smirk for Taranee and a wink for Hay Lin.

And for Cornelia? Peter flashed the most adorable smile she'd seen all day.

It was so adorable Cornelia suddenly felt as though her feet had turned into balloons. The skin at her hairline prickled with sudden sweat. Cornelia found herself fantasizing about jumping into Peter's car, snuggling up with him, and taking a long, cozy trip through the rain.

And much to Cornelia's surprise, that was just what Peter was offering.

"Hi!" he cried, through the noise of the storm. "Hop in, if you can manage to find some room between my surfboards."

Cornelia peered past Peter into the station wagon. The surfboards' tails were tucked into the wagon's way-back, their middles bisecting the backseat and their tips resting up front, at Peter's elbow. The sight of the big boards pretty

21

much destroyed Cornelia's front-seat snuggling fantasy. Then again, they *inspired* visions of Peter Cook surfing, and that was just as good. Cornelia immediately found herself falling into a daydream of Peter at the beach. His cute dreads were wet from the spray of saltwater, and he was looking *very* nice in a bathing sui—

"Hay Lin and I will get in back," Taranee announced, jolting Cornelia out of her reverie. "Cornelia, why don't you hop in front?"

Cornelia's eyes widened.

Her breath quickened.

Then she blurted out the only answer that she could possibly think of.

"No!"

Peter's eyebrows shot up.

Great, Cornelia thought in a panic. Now he thinks I'm a total freak! Time for a quick cover-up.

"I mean . . . I can't," she said with a shrug and a high-pitched giggle. She opened her big, purple umbrella and ducked under its shelter gratefully. "I have to . . . um . . . run an errand. For my mother."

"No problem," Peter said, with a sweet smile. "I'll take you. Where do you need to go?"

Could Peter be *any* nicer? Cornelia thought with a frustrated groan. This wasn't going well at all!

"I need to walk there, actually," she declared. "To a . . . a relative's house, which is right near here."

Cornelia looked at Taranee and Hay Lin, who'd both clambered into the backseat by then. They were gazing at her with confused expressions.

"I'll see you at Irma's, okay?" she called to them.

"Sure," her friends said in unison. They glanced at each other conspiratorially. Taranee looked suspicious. Hay Lin was shrugging in exaggerated bewilderment.

Cornelia almost grunted with impatience. She could just hear them whispering to each other after they drove off.

"I didn't know Cornelia had relatives in the neighborhood," Taranee would say to Hay Lin.

"All I know," Hay Lin would reply with one of her impish grins, "is that she gets very peculiar when she's around your *brother*."

Speaking of which, the boy himself was talking again! Cornelia had to focus.

"So . . . see you around some time?" Peter said.

As Peter offered those hopeful words, Cornelia felt a little zing shoot through her. If it weren't raining, she was sure her fine, blond hair would be standing on end!

As it was, Cornelia was just dry-mouthed and absolutely stumped for a clever comeback. The most amusing reply she could muster was, "Sure thing, Peter! See you soon. And say hi to your folks for me."

Aaaigh!

The moment those words left her mouth, Cornelia winced. Could she have sounded any lamer?

At least Peter's trying to pretend he doesn't notice, she thought with a groan.

Peter was indeed giving her another friendly wave. Weakly, she waved back as Peter drove off in his car with Taranee and Hay Lin cozily tucked into the backseat.

"Say hi to your folks?" Cornelia muttered to herself as she began to walk down the rainy sidewalk. "Did I really just say that? What was I thinking? I'm completely embarrassed!"

She was becoming confused.

Why, she wailed inwardly, am I getting all these crushy feelings about Peter? I mean, I like him. But I *love* Caleb.

Even at the thought of that name, Cornelia felt another wave of emotion wash over her. She went jelly-legged, and her face flushed. Beneath the swoon, though, something much deeper was happening. She was recalling the brief moment—both exquisite and unspeakably painful—that she had met her love, Caleb.

How had this brown-haired boy of her dreams become hers?

Well, for starters, Cornelia thought, I dreamed of him long before I ever met him. My visions of Caleb were the first hint of magic I ever felt.

Cornelia felt a stab of longing as she remembered the first time she had "seen" him. She'd been daydreaming her way through a boring science class, gazing at a fluffy treetop just outside her classroom window. Suddenly, the leaves had begun fluttering and shifting—until they'd formed a picture. It was Caleb! Not that Cornelia knew his name then. She only knew he was the most beautiful boy she'd ever seen, and that he had to be her soul mate.

After that vision, Caleb began showing up all over the place. In Cornelia's dreams; in the absentminded doodles she drew in the margins of her notebooks; even in Elyon's sketchbook. Elyon had drawn Caleb for Cornelia back when she'd just seemed an ordinary earth girl—and Cornelia's best friend.

Cornelia continued to reminisce as she meandered down the street, hunched under her umbrella.

She'd met Caleb in person the last time she'd crossed through a portal to get to Metamoor. The portal had culminated in the depths of a stone fountain in the middle of one of Meridian's Gothic plazas. Cornelia had found herself too far below the water's surface, desperate for air, and fearing for her life! Just before she'd sunk into unconsciousness, a strong hand had reached into the water and grabbed her. It had pulled Cornelia upward to the spot where she'd emerged, gasping, from the water. When she saw who'd saved her life, she'd lost her breath all over again.

It was the boy of her dreams.

Cornelia's dream boy turned out to be real! Unfortunately, he was also risking his life every day. He was leading a band of Metamoorian rebels, fighting against Phobos's brutal army, in order to help restore Elyon to the throne.

So, almost as quickly as they'd met, Cornelia and Caleb had said good-bye. They had both had their own battles to fight in their own worlds.

Before he had bid her farewell, though, Caleb had confided something to Cornelia—he'd been dreaming about *her* as well. He loved her, too.

The moment had been so bittersweet that strong, independent Cornelia had wept. Caleb had caught one of her tears on his fingertip. Using his Metamoorian magic, he'd transformed the salty droplet into a glowing, silver flower—a magic memento that Cornelia kept in a vase on her desk at home. It was the last thing she gazed at before drifting off to sleep each night and the first thing she spotted when she opened her eyes each morning.

As Cornelia continued to walk down the darkening street, her thoughts drifted to Elyon, whose absence was so confounding.

Ever since they'd been little girls, Cornelia and Elyon had been best friends. Elyon had been sweet, boy-crazy, and just a little bit shy. She was as petite as Cornelia was tall. Both girls had long, blond hair and otherworldly imaginations. Elyon had been Cornelia's biggest fan at the skating rink, and Cornelia had always been there to comfort Elyon when she'd gotten a bad grade or developed a crush on a boy.

Elyon was different then, Cornelia thought with a shaky sigh. Before she discovered her true powers. Before she became . . . our enemy.

Former enemy, now, Cornelia thought.

Of all the Guardians, Cornelia alone had never believed that Elyon was truly bad. She'd insisted that Elyon had been deceived by the evil Cedric.

Now, it seemed that Cornelia might have been right. Lately, Elyon was questioning her loyalty to Cedric and beginning to reach out to the Guardians more frequently.

But Elyon's still so far away, Cornelia brooded as she walked. My best friend *and* Caleb are both beyond the Veil, in Meridian. I wonder how Elyon knew years ago, that one day I'd meet him. Could she have invented Caleb? Or maybe she saw him somewhere before?

As Cornelia walked on, the pensive rhythm of her own footsteps was somehow soothing, lulling her into deeper and deeper reflection about Elyon's mysterious role as Metamoorian royalty.

Did Elyon know all along that she was the Light of Meridian? Cornelia wondered. Or was drawing her way of seeing Meridian, the place where she was born, without even knowing it?

Yes, Cornelia decided. That's it! It was Elyon's drawing that connected her to her native land. Drawing was her way of moving through barriers, like the Veil, without completely realizing it.

Elyon, thought Cornelia, has built a bridge between our two worlds!

THREE

Fruuuuush, hummed the rain shower.

At least, that's what it did in Elyon's imagination—and on the parchment spread out on her ornate, gold-trimmed desk. With a craggy, oversized pencil in the shape of a twig, Elyon was sketching raindrops streaming onto a city street, spattering against cement, and glistening in the glow of a streetlamp.

It wasn't Metamoor she was drawing. In this world—the world that she now knew as her birthplace and her destiny—the weather was always the same. It never rained. Then again, the sun never shone, either. The leaves on the trees never withered, and the only flowers that thrived were in the mystical garden of Elyon's brother, Prince Phobos.

Protected by a thorny thicket of poisonous, black roses, the garden was beautiful. Even more stunning was the secret grove where Phobos's Murmurers lived.

Like blooms that had come to life, those creatures' complexions ranged from blue to purple to iridescent pink. Their hair trailed on the ground behind them, undulating like sea plants. They spoke in whispers, and were the eyes and ears of Phobos. Anything a Murmurer saw, Phobos saw, too. Anything a Murmurer heard, Phobos heard. Anything Phobos wanted to have said, the Murmurers said. They told him what they saw and heard in the streets of Meridian, in people's homes, even in Phobos's own castle.

The Murmurers were like a part of Phobos.

When Elyon had first come to Metamoor, her brother's lieutenant, Cedric, had explained all of that to her. He'd told her about the dangers and burdens of the royal life. It had made sense at the time, when she'd been confused, angry, and hurt because her parents had lied to her.

My *adoptive* parents, Elyon corrected herself. The ones who stole me away from my home and hid my true identity from me.

As she shaded in another rippling rain

puddle in her drawing, Elyon couldn't help wondering about something.

Maybe they took me away to give me a better life in Heatherfield, she thought. A world with sunshine and rain, with a house and a school, instead of this looming, lonely fortress.

Elyon tried to shake those thoughts from her head.

Such ideas are useless, she scolded herself. Metamoor is my life now. It's the life I chose. . . .

Elyon's head began to ache as more questions began to surface in her mind. She wondered about the Metamoorian people, with their sad faces, hunched shoulders, and rough, brown cloaks that were so different from Elyon's own ice-blue, silken robes.

She wondered about her adoptive parents, huddled in a prison cell. They were within walking distance of the palace, but, at the same time, seemed so far away.

Elyon bent closer to her paper, trying to find comfort in the familiar scratching of her pencil, in the memories coming to life through her art.

"What are you drawing, Elyon?"

Elyon's spine stiffened.

How does he do it? she wondered without

turning to see who was speaking to her from the doorway. She already knew.

Cedric always seems to sense it when I'm dreaming of home or when I'm thinking of my old life, Elyon lamented silently. That's when he shows up to drag me back to Meridian and my new life.

"I'm drawing rain, Cedric," Elyon answered dully, still not looking at him. "It reminds of me of some afternoons in Heatherfield."

"But you aren't a silly Heatherfield girl any longer," Cedric chided Elyon. He strode into her room. Elyon sensed him coming over to stand behind her chair. She could tell from his smooth voice that Cedric was in his human, rather than his giant, serpentine form. She remembered when she'd thought Cedric's chiseled cheekbones, razorlike jaw, and long, pale hair were completely cute.

That seemed like a lifetime ago. Now, Elyon found Cedric less appealing every time she looked at him—and every time he nagged her, as he was doing right now.

"You're the ruler of Meridian," Cedric declared.

"Right!" Elyon laughed. "Like in a bizarre

fairy tale that has an ending I don't know."

"Fairy tales are useless inventions," Cedric said matter-of-factly.

With a sigh of frustration, Elyon tossed her pencil onto her marble desktop. She couldn't possibly draw with Cedric hovering over her. She flounced out of her chair and glanced at Cedric before striding to the balcony of her bedroom—a round platform overlooking a vast Metamoorian valley. The landscape was edged by mountains. Smoke billowing from chimneys around the medieval city made the air gray and murky.

"You think fairy tales are useless, huh?" Elyon said coldly over her shoulder. At his dismissive response, she turned her back upon him again. Gazing out over the war-torn city, she said, "My parents used to tell me fairy tales, and I loved to draw them. 'Once upon a time, there was a little queen who reigned over a sad, dreary world. . . .'"

Reacting instantly, Cedric rushed to Elyon's side, his long, blue robes flapping around his knees.

"Your parents?" he spat. "You mean those traitors who kidnapped you."

"Cedric! Enough!" Elyon said. She tried to infuse her voice with anger and authority, but instead, it merely quivered, as thin and plaintive as a little girl's. Elyon knew that pain was flickering across her face as well. She didn't want Cedric to see this moment of weakness, so she tucked her chin into her chest and pushed past him, returning to her bedroom.

Elyon didn't feel like a queen. She just felt confused—more and more confused with each day she spent in this cold castle.

"You realize that what they did to you was terrible, right?" Cedric declared.

I don't realize it! Elyon cried silently. You have realized it for me. I don't know what to believe.

"Stop it!" she rasped, refusing to meet Cedric's eyes.

He did not—would not—obey.

"It's because of your 'parents' that your brother, Prince Phobos, suffered for so long," Cedric continued. "The people had lost all their hope. And the land its light. Furthermore . . ."

Cedric's rant pounded at Elyon as her many questions continued to torment her from within. She felt her shoulders tighten. Heat and anger flushed her pale cheeks. Elyon sensed flashes of white magic sparking from her fingertips.

She couldn't take one more second of Cedric's voice! Her vision suddenly went red with rage.

"*I said, stop it!*" she screamed.

Elyon spun to glare at Cedric. Her long braids, bound at the ends by two heavy, wooden rings, whipped around her face. Beneath her feet, she felt a slight rumbling. She was so angry.

"You don't know my parents!" she shouted at Cedric. "You can't talk about them like that!"

Ruummmmmble!

Cedric suddenly stumbled backward, then gaped at the floor.

Elyon blinked.

Wait a minute, she thought. The palace really is shifting and shuddering. And it seems to be scaring Cedric to death!

That, of course, was immensely satisfying to Elyon. Cedric's cold, smooth-skinned face froze in terror. He stared at Elyon in fearful wonder as he struggled to keep his balance.

Elyon would have laughed if she hadn't been so enraged.

He thinks *I* did this? she scoffed as she stiffened her legs, bracing herself to keep her balance. Ridiculous! He doesn't know anything. He also thinks my parents are *evil*. He's been filling my head with such anger, such *ugliness*. I can't *take it anymore*!

Rummmmmmmble!!!

The floor quaked again, knocking Cedric off his feet. He slithered backward, cringing, as chunks of plaster plummeted from the bedroom's high ceiling, hitting the marble floor with harsh *thunk*s.

"I . . . I . . ." Cedric stuttered at Elyon. "Forgive me!"

"Forgive?" Elyon barked. "You? But I don't really know you, do I?"

"That hurts me, Elyon," Cedric declared as he crouched on the floor. "I'm the only person you can trust completely."

Suddenly, Elyon's rage evaporated. In its place a heavy cloud of dejection filled her heart.

At the same time, she noticed vaguely, the rumbling beneath her feet died away. The floor stopped shifting. The earthquake had ended.

Elyon moved back onto her balcony.

Leaning against the doorway, she gazed out at the smoke-marred landscape.

"Oh, really?" she answered Cedric dully. "I can trust you, can I? Fine. Then tell me where my home is. Because it's not the one out there."

Elyon clutched harder at the doorway as grief rose up within her. A tear trembled on her eyelashes for a moment before falling onto her blue tunic.

"I used to have a mother and father," Elyon whispered. "I had friends and—"

"But then you didn't have a kingdom to take care of."

Elyon glanced over her shoulder. Cedric wasn't speaking. Somebody else had entered her room. It was her brother, Phobos.

He was looming in her bedroom doorway, looking very royal. His robe was a vivid color of turquoise, topped with a snowy white, velvet cowl. Two Murmurers floated behind him, making sure his robe's billowing train never touched the floor.

Phobos's long hair had been spun into vine-like twists of endless, glossy braids. The braids extended from his proud head in every direction.

"Don't worry, Elyon," Phobos continued. Though Cedric threw himself at Phobos's feet, muttering an obsequious greeting, Phobos ignored him. His attention was focused on Elyon. "I'm here for you, and nothing is stronger than the bond between brother and sister."

Elyon nodded sadly. Phobos's blue eyes narrowed. He glanced away from his frail sister to Cedric, who cowered before him.

"Would you like Cedric to leave forever, my dear sister?" Phobos asked, glaring down at his henchman.

"N—no," Elyon said. She hated that word—forever. It had been the word she'd used when she'd defected to Metamoor.

Good-bye forever was what she had thought when she'd left her home, when she'd watched her parents being hauled off to prison.

"I'm just so confused!" Elyon cried. "I'll speak to Cedric later."

Elyon sighed with relief as she watched Phobos walk over and talk to Cedric under his breath. Phobos looked furious.

"Yes, my lord," Cedric squeaked before scuttling out of the room.

Elyon turned to the window. She gazed out across the rooftops and tree branches again. But this time, she focused on a hulking building, looming atop a mountain peak about a mile away. Elyon felt a stab of guilt as she gazed at the structure. It was Metamoor's prison.

Her parents' prison.

Now, it was her brother who glided up behind her. She felt rather than heard him, because he moved with utter silence.

She angled her head.

"Phobos?" she said. "I'm the Light of Meridian, right?"

"That is the title that awaits you," her brother confirmed in a deep, soothing voice. "The title that will soon be yours."

"I spoke with my parents," Elyon admitted. "My adoptive parents in prison. I would like to grant them their freedom."

"Ah," Phobos said. Elyon cocked her head the other way. Did she detect a trace of tension in Phobos's voice as it rang out behind her?

"A wise decision," Phobos said. He was smiling down at her, his arms open wide in a welcoming gesture.

"You'll only have to wait a little while longer," Phobos said. "The power of your future dynasty is handed down from female to female. I will gladly relinquish the burden of the crown to you."

Which means, Elyon thought elatedly, I'll be able to do whatever I want—including releasing my parents without asking for Phobos's permission. She almost jumped for joy, but her brother's dignified presence inhibited her. It was hard to imagine that the stately Phobos ever jumped for joy. Or swung from a tree branch. Or played, at all.

That must be how he became so wise, Elyon decided. Not to mention, aloof.

Phobos began to leave, gliding back across Elyon's room. His Murmurers flitted just ahead of their master to open the doors.

As he slid through the doorway, Phobos called over his shoulder, "Unfortunately, you will be able to assume full powers only after the official coronation ceremony. You understand, don't you?"

"The coronation," she repeated. "When is that?"

"Soon, my dear sister," Phobos said. "Very

soon." Without another word, he swept into the hallway and left Elyon alone once again.

Thump!

The fancy glass doors swung shut.

The coronation will solve everything, Elyon thought. Even if they aren't my real parents, I still care about them. I'm glad that we can get everything straightened out soon.

She perched dreamily at the edge of her grand, gilded bed. Like everything else in Elyon's quarters, the bed dwarfed her. It was the polar opposite of the bed of her childhood memories, a twin mattress draped with a fleecy, pink bedspread and ruffly little pillows.

Elyon could picture that bed more vividly than the one right beneath her. Sitting on it, in Elyon's fantasy, was her sweet-faced, red-haired mother, nestled between Elyon's old stuffed animals.

Suddenly, Elyon rushed headlong into a memory. She was no longer the royal Elyon, teenage queen-to-be. She was five-year-old Elyon, scrambling around the floor of her room in her favorite orange overalls.

Elyon held a fat crayon in each fist as she

stopped to gaze up at her mother. Her mother was looking at her latest drawing—a picture the girl had been laboring over all morning. Somehow, Elyon hadn't been able to get the picture quite right.

Her mother frowned as she studied the drawing.

Anxiously, Elyon squeaked, "Why are you sad, Mommy? Don't you like the city I drew?"

Elyon scrambled up next to her mother and peeked at the city's stone turrets and thatched-roof cottages. Flags of every color were strung between the rooftops. Flying above everything was a winged girl with a crown.

"I'm not sad," Elyon's mother told her. "It's just that your drawing reminds me of a place I used to know, many, many years ago. And that girl who's flying . . ."

"I know," Elyon sighed, crossing her arms over her chest with a sigh. "It's bad. I wanted her to light up the whole sky, just like the sun. Instead, I messed up all the colors. And I can't draw faces, either!"

Elyon felt herself get all choked up. Her lower lip trembled.

Her mother reached down and scooped up

an eraser. Elyon loved that pink eraser. It was her favorite color and it smelled like bubble gum.

"You can just erase it all," Elyon's mom said, holding up the eraser with a smile. "See this?"

Elyon nodded.

Whish-whish-whish . . .

Her mother whisked the eraser over the paper with a few sure, quick strokes. The ugly princess's face was gone! Now there was just a nice, white spot in the middle of the drawing— the perfect place to try again.

"Now you try," her mother prompted, placing the eraser into Elyon's chubby little fingers. "With one stroke of your hand, you can erase any mistake."

Elyon waved her hand in the air, giving the erasing motion a try.

Startled, she blinked. Her hand was no longer dimpled and tiny, bathed in Heatherfield sunshine. It was now draped in the long sleeve of her Metamoorian robe.

Her fantasy had evaporated as quickly as her temper tantrum had. Elyon, the future queen, was back.

Only one thing remained from her day-dream—a surge of hope.

"My mom will explain everything to me," she whispered to herself as she gazed out her window once more at the prison. "She used to explain things so well. She was so good at that sort of thing."

On impulse, Elyon hugged herself, wrapping her arms around her body, the way she'd done as a child whenever she'd felt content—when she'd made a good drawing, when there'd been chocolate ice cream for dessert, when she'd had a play date with Cornelia.

Remember, Elyon, she could hear her mother say, *you can erase any mistake.*

FOUR

Shaaatzzzzzz!

"Aaaaiiighhhhh!"

Cedric tried to contain his scream when the Murmurer prodded him. The effort was useless. The yellow-and-green-striped creature had jabbed viciously at his shoulder blade, sending a searing jolt down his arm.

Collapsing to the ground of Phobos's garden, Cedric looked at his clenched hand. No, his fingers were still there. They were no longer the pale, elegant digits of his human hand, though. In his agony, Cedric had not been able to hold on to his alternate form. He had reverted to his Metamoorian shape—green and slimy, with a red mask over his eyes and a slithery tail in place of legs.

The Murmurer's torture left him curled up on the ground in pain, clawing at the dirt and gazing beseechingly toward a steaming, hot spring.

Bathing in that spring was Prince Phobos. The handsome young man lolled arrogantly in the fragrant, bubbling water.

I deserve this, Cedric thought with a low whimper. I endangered my master's secret, his entire plan for Elyon! In doing so, I also endangered my own life.

Shaatttzzzz!

Cedric shrieked loudly as the malevolent Murmurer stabbed again at Cedric's back. The little imp snickered as Cedric cowered and wept.

Please, my lord, my prince, Cedric begged silently. Have mercy on me, your faithful servant. I've lied for you. Always willingly. For I have had faith that you will someday elevate me to something beyond this wretched body, beyond my mere serpenthood.

Cedric wished he could have declared all of those things to Prince Phobos. He knew, though, that Phobos would have refused him any show of remorse.

It was too late for such declarations.

That was confirmed when Phobos finally deigned to speak.

"You've made a huge mistake, Cedric," he said. His voice was lazy, lulled by the fragrant oils of his hot bath. The words were casual, but true evil lurked beneath them. Cedric respected that power as much as he feared it.

"You've instilled doubt in Elyon," Phobos continued, his blue eyes narrowing. "Her faith is beginning to waver, and that is *not* a good thing."

"I . . . I don't understand," Cedric gasped, his voice becoming shrill. "She's always believed in me and in what I have told her."

"Things have changed," Phobos said. He shifted angrily, sending a spray of bubbles to the surface of the spring. "The sign was clear. You felt her rage as well, didn't you?"

"Are you talking about that tremor?" Cedric whined, remembering how afraid he'd been earlier, when the floor of Elyon's bedroom had shifted beneath his feet. At the moment, however, he'd have given anything for that to have been due to a simple earthquake!

But . . . did Phobos believe that Elyon had

caused Metamoor's shudder? That would make her almost as powerful as Phobos himself. It couldn't be! Cedric could not stop himself—he spoke his concern out loud.

"But, my lord," he declared, "she isn't powerful enough to—"

"She's more powerful than any of us!" Phobos raged, beating at the water with his fists. Instinctively, the Murmurers attacked Cedric, taking Phobos's frustration out on his loyal servant.

Shaaatttzzz! They directed pain to his chest.

Shaaatttzzz! They directed pain to his tail.

Shaaatttzzz! They directed pain to his ear, sending more waves of pain shooting through his reptilian head. For a moment, he was blinded.

I must learn to keep quiet, he thought as he gasped and heaved.

"Her power is dormant now, but it will show itself soon," Phobos continued. He stood up suddenly. As always, his flitting servants had anticipated his action. Two Murmurers darted forward to drape the man's slim body in a gossamer cloth. A third presented him with a bowl of glistening nectar. Phobos delicately dipped his hands into the nectar, covering his skin with its beautifying solution.

As the Murmurers ministered to him, Phobos gazed down at Cedric.

"Because of you, we now risk seeing her gain her full powers before it is time," Phobos declared.

Cedric cowered at his master's bare feet.

Forgive . . . he begged silently. Forgive . . .

"If those two officers hadn't kidnapped her when she was a baby," Phobos raged on, "I would have already absorbed her energy by now. Those traitors and that nurse, Galgheita, took my sister to earth. They wanted to keep her hidden away from me."

At that statement, Cedric cocked his head. Though remorseful, he *was* still a snake. And, like any cold-blooded creature, he could smell an opportunity when it approached.

Phobos was musing out loud, letting Cedric in on his plan. That meant one of two things: either Phobos was planning to harm Cedric—to fill his head with tantalizing plans before he silenced him forever—or . . . Phobos needed Cedric's help.

This is a chance to redeem myself, Cedric

thought, running his dry, forked tongue over his green lips.

He struggled to his feet.

I have to display confidence, not cowardice, he told himself. My life may depend upon it.

"Now," Phobos was saying, "to absorb Elyon's vital force, I'll have to overcome stronger barriers."

"How will you do that, my lord?"

"At the coronation ceremony, Cedric," Phobos declared. At those words, the Murmurers draped a regal robe around Phobos's strong shoulders. "There, Elyon will wear the crown for the first—and last—time. Until then, the two prisoners mustn't speak with her!"

Cedric's hands had stopped trembling. He recognized what was coming—a task that would surely involve plotting and stealth.

It would be my pleasure to help, Cedric thought. His pained grimace slowly morphed into a smarmy grin as he spoke up.

"An 'accident' could befall them in prison, my lord," Cedric proposed with a humble bow. "Elyon will never suspect a thing."

"Excellent!" Phobos said with an evil smile.

"If you do a good job, you may come with me to the Abyss of Shadows, and there, you may drink from the legendary black spring."

Cedric stifled a gasp.

The black spring! he thought.

The tarlike substance that bubbled from the ground deep in Phobos's garden comprised Metamoor's very essence. Concentrated in that spring was all of the energy Phobos had absorbed from Metamoor's atmosphere, its natural resources, and its inhabitants' very souls. It was the epicenter of Phobos's beautiful garden, a shelter from the harsh world that he himself had created.

This is the ultimate honor, Cedric thought breathlessly. He was relieved to see Phobos turn his back on him and stride silently away. That meant Cedric was safe for the moment.

Prince Phobos is pleased with me, Cedric thought as he gazed after his departing master. The lives of Elyon's parents are certainly worth that!

Just before Phobos left Cedric's line of vision, he turned to walk down a petal-strewn path. For a split second, Cedric spied Phobos's face.

There wasn't a trace of earnestness in it.

Instead, Phobos's expression was twisted and scheming.

Cedric recognized that look. It was one he'd often worn himself when teasing Elyon or manipulating Metamoorian soldiers into doing his will.

But in the haze of his pain—which had been followed so quickly by elation—Cedric failed to connect Phobos's sinister countenance with his own fate. All Cedric knew was that his master had allowed him back into his favor. He'd graced him with his mercy. He'd tantalized Cedric with the promise of the black spring and its transformative powers.

Cedric grinned as he imagined his green scales and inelegant tail replaced by a glinting, amphibious skin of purple and gold.

He dreamed of a life purely devoted to serving Phobos.

"Soon, I, too," Cedric whispered, "will live in the palace as a Murmurer!"

FIVE

Irma peeked out her kitchen window and scowled.

Could this day be *any* worse? she wondered with a groan. My friends are all late for dinner. And there's a nasty surprise waiting for them *at* dinner.

An angry thunderclap rumbled through the sky. For some reason, that sound—a temper tantrum of the heavens if she'd ever heard one—made Irma think about Metamoor.

Yes, she thought morosely. This dreary, rainy day totally reminds me of Metamoor. The sky is always gray there and the air always feels heavy. It's ugly and noisy and—

Wheeeeee!

Irma glanced behind her at the unpleasant

sound. The pressure cooker was whistling like mad!

Wheeeeeeee!

"Mom!" Irma yelped, turning away from the window to scan the kitchen for her maternal unit. Unfortunately, the only family member around was Irma's annoying younger brother, Christopher. He was sitting on a stool at the kitchen counter, playing war with the salt and pepper shakers. He liked to pretend the shakers were battling each other, and would move them around as if they were soldiers.

The shrieking pressure cooker was getting louder and louder. She couldn't focus on Christopher's soldiers—or *any* of the chaos going on at the Lair house.

"The pressure cooker is whistling!" Irma called out as the whistle became, if possible, even shriller.

Irma's mom poked her head out of the pantry.

"So, it's whistling," she shrugged, obviously not bothered by the noise. "All you need to do is sing, Irma. Then we'll have a nice chorus going."

"Hee-hee!" Christopher giggled. "A nice little chorus! Hee!"

Irma scowled.

"Now I know why we have Christopher," Irma told her mother drily. "You needed someone to laugh at your jokes."

"Of course," Mom said. She deftly threw some spices into a large pot on the stove with one hand, lowered the flame under the pressure cooker with the other, then called over her shoulder, "Hand me the salt, would you, please?"

Irma could easily have grabbed the salt from Christopher and handed it to her mother. But first, she wanted to sneak a peek over her mom's shoulder to see what was bubbling in the various pots and pans on the stove.

It was a bad idea. The first pot she spotted revealed a horror!

"You made zucchini!" Irma yelped. "But I told you, Cornelia doesn't like zucchini!"

"So?" Christopher taunted from behind Mom's skirt. "*You* don't like Cornelia!"

Irma's eyes widened. Christopher had a point. Irma and Corny (as Irma liked to refer to Cornelia, just to get a rise out of her) had their differences. Just like their elements, water and earth, they were totally different.

Hey, can I help it if Cornelia's got no sense of humor? Irma thought huffily.

But Irma and Cornelia had been friends for a long time. Even though they were very different, now that they were both Guardians, they had to work together no matter *how* much they annoyed each other. The fate of the world depended on it!

Irma had been trying—trying!—to be a little more grown-up lately. That meant no more turning feisty boys into toads, no more using her magic to cheat at quizzes in school, and no more baiting Cornelia. And she had to admit, most of the time, she actually enjoyed Corny's company.

Not that Christopher needed to know that! Irma was *not* about to give her nosy brat of a brother a victory.

"What do you know about it, squirt?" she asked. "So, Cornelia and I have had a few arguments. So what?"

Mom glanced up from her cooking.

"Christopher," she scolded, "don't say mean things. Especially when we have company over."

Mom turned back to her cooking, giving

Christopher the opening he needed in order to stick his tongue out at Irma. Irma was on the verge of making a retort when her mom spun back around.

"Speaking of company," Mrs. Lair declared, "Christopher, take these appetizers into the dining room. Our guests must be hungry."

Irma snickered as Christopher scowled. Morosely, he took the tray from his mother and headed into the dining room.

Good, Irma thought. Little Mr. Buttinsky is out of my hair. Now I can focus on our surprise guests. I have to warn my friends before they come inside. Of course, that'll never happen if they don't get here in the first place!

Irma blew a wisp of hair out of her blue eyes and peered out the window again.

This time, she saw two figures hunched over in the rain, stomping up her front walk. Immediately, Irma recognized Hay Lin's marshmallowlike white parka and Taranee's woolly hat.

"Yes!" Irma whispered, hurrying out of the kitchen. "I can hit two Guardians with one stone."

Irma was just about to open the front door

when she noticed a third person splashing up the walk.

"Hey, wait up!"

"Will!" Taranee cried.

"Look who's here," Hay Lin added. "But why the sad, puppy-dog face?"

"*Don't* talk about animals, okay?" Will answered with a groan.

Hmmm, Irma thought with a sneaky grin. This sounds juicy. I'll just listen in for a second.

Imagining the suave sleuth on *Spygirl*, her second-favorite TV show after *Boy Comet*, Irma pressed an ear to the door. Her friends' voices were carrying through quite nicely.

Now, if only I had one of Spygirl's cool wigs, Irma thought.

"Oooh!" That was Hay Lin's giggly voice. Irma listened closely.

"Something tells me," Hay Lin continued, "we'd better avoid any topic related to animals and Matt."

Matt! Irma thought. Will's way-cute crush? What happened?

"Ha-ha!" Will grumbled at Hay Lin. "Very funny . . . but true. Everything was a total disaster at the pet shop. But the worst thing happened back at my house afterward. Mom said we had to talk about something 'very important.' With Mr. Collins!"

Oh, wow, Irma thought. Whatever happened with Will's mom, who was dating a Sheffield history teacher, was definitely big news. Irma knew that Will was not very happy about the situation.

"I'm so glad I had an excuse to get out of there," Will sighed to her friends. "Irma's dinner invitation was the perfect excuse to leave."

Taranee, the voice of reason, as always, piped up, "But why? Didn't you say Mr. Collins was getting to be almost nice?"

"There's a huge difference," Will protested, "between a nice guy and a father!"

"Oh, come on!" Hay Lin cried.

Irma could just picture Hay Lin's eyes becoming wide and questioning.

"You think they wanted to tell you they're engaged? Isn't it a little soon for something like that?" Hay Lin asked.

Way soon, Irma thought with a nod. Mr. Collins and Mrs. Vandom have only been dating for, like, a minute. Hey! Speaking of minutes, I have maybe one before my mom starts hollering at me to serve our guests some fancy hors d'oeuvres. Our *guests!* Ugh!

Feeling a fluttering in her belly, Irma finally grabbed the doorknob and peeked out at her rain-soaked friends.

"Sorry to interrupt," she said in a stage whisper, "but we have a little problem in here."

"Huh?" Hay Lin cried, surprised.

"What is it?" Will asked.

Putting a finger to her lips, Irma looked to her left, her right, and behind her. Then she hurried her friends into the bathroom. As she pressed the door shut behind them all, Irma tried to come up with just the right words to tell her fellow Guardians the big news—they wouldn't be dining alone tonight!

Instead, she thought, our supper will be filled with intrigue. And danger!

"Uh . . . Irma?" Will squeaked, breaking in to Irma's thoughts. Irma surfaced from her daydream and blinked at her friends. Will was sitting on the side of the tub, while Taranee and Hay Lin were jostling for room on the edge of the vanity. They did *not* look very comfortable.

The time has come, Irma thought dramatically. I must reveal the truth!

"Here's the story," she began. "You'll never guess who's sitting in my dining room at this very moment. . . ."

Fifteen minutes later, Irma peered out her window again. She'd been peeking out every sixty seconds or so, ever since her mother had ushered her edgy friends in to the dining room to join the guests.

Finally, Irma's constant check-ins paid off! She spotted Cornelia making her way across the street toward Irma's front door. Under her umbrella, Cornelia looked bothered.

Irma opened the front door, then glanced over her shoulder at the arched entryway to the dining room. Smatterings of polite conversation and the clink of cocktail glasses were drifting out into the hallway. The crowd was ready to eat. But if Irma didn't first fill Cornelia in on two specific members of that crowd, she'd be in big trouble.

Which means, Irma thought, Cornelia needs to hurry up! I'll just give her a little help.

Irma thrust her arms through the front door. She felt a stirring in her chest as magic began to well up within her. The cool, fluid energy bubbled up into her shoulders, down her arms, and finally out of her fingertips, in the form of a swirly blue ray.

The stream of magic shot out into the rain, dancing between the drops like a playful snake. In its wake, the snake left a dry pathway, creating a rain-free passageway for Cornelia to walk through.

Cornelia peeked out incredulously from beneath her umbrella. When she spotted Irma at the end of the dry path, she grinned. Closing her umbrella with an efficient snap, Cornelia began to hurry toward her friend.

Perfect, Irma thought. Now I can talk to Corny before anyone inter—

"Who is it?"

"Yikes!" Irma yelped, glancing behind her at the intruder. It was Christopher! That little brat! Irma immediately dropped her hands to her sides, flicking away any traces of blue energy.

Frussssshhh!

Whoops! Irma thought, cringing. That sounds an awful lot like rain resuming. Slowly, she turned back to the doorway.

Yup. Without Irma's magical interference to protect her, Cornelia had been thoroughly doused. She stood on the path for a moment, glaring at Irma through soaked strands of long, blond hair. Then she slogged irritably up the front steps and into the foyer.

"Hi, Cornelia," Christopher piped up. "You're soaking wet. Why didn't you use your umbrella?"

"Well, I really didn't think I needed one," Cornelia replied, with another icy stare at Irma. "A second ago, that is. Is everything okay, Irma?"

"Of course!" Irma said in a loud, fake voice. "Come right in."

Okay, Irma thought. I just have to act like a normal person welcoming a friend to my house, and nobody will suspect that I'm actually harboring *dire* news. I just have to get Cornelia alone!

"Well!" Irma called out again, coating her voice with sugar. "Since you're soaking wet, let's go to my room and get you some dry clothes."

Cornelia raised one eyebrow at Irma, then leaned down and whispered to Christopher, "What's gotten into your sister?"

"Dunno!" Christopher whispered back with

an evil grin. "I've been wondering that my whole life!"

Oooh, Irma thought, clenching her fists. Christopher is *sooo* annoying. I'll deal with him later. First, I've got to—

"Cornelia! Could you come in here for a minute?"

Eeek! Irma thought. It's my dad. And when Sergeant Lair issues orders, no one turns him down.

"There are some people I'd like you to meet," her dad continued.

Yeah, Irma thought desperately. Some *scheming* people.

"Coming, Mr. Lair!" Cornelia said. She was oblivious to Irma's frantic look as she pulled her wet poncho up over her head and hung it on the coatrack.

Cornelia began to walk toward the dining room.

Noooooo! Irma cried silently. She grabbed Cornelia's arm.

Cornelia responded with a scowl that clearly said, "What's *up* with you?" She shook Irma off and proceeded into the dining room.

Helplessly, Irma followed. Her friend had

come to an abrupt halt next to Irma's dad at the end of the dining room table. Seated around an elaborate dinner spread were Hay Lin, Will, and Taranee, all flashing too-bright, highly uncomfortable smiles. Through their fake grins, they were glancing shiftily at the two people sitting at the table's far end: a stocky little woman in round glasses and a rock-jawed man with probing, blue eyes. The strangers were wearing matching blue blazers.

Government-issue blue blazers, to be specific, Irma thought.

"So, Cornelia," her dad was saying in a booming voice. "I don't need to introduce you to your friends, obviously. But I don't think you know Agents Medina and McTiennan."

"They work for Interpol!" Irma exclaimed. "And they're *not* here on vacation!"

"Irma!" Dad sputtered. He turned on his daughter with a face Irma totally recognized. It was his if-we-weren't-in-the-presence-of-company-I'd-give-you-a-lecture face. He was all business.

Irma hesitated.

What would Spygirl do in a situation like this? she wondered. Would she be a good girl and keep her mouth shut? Or would she risk it all—life, limb, and this week's allowance—to impart essential information to a friend in need?

Irma squared her shoulders.

It's a no-brainer! she thought. I have to do whatever it takes to tell Corny what these *agents* are doing—

"Let me tell you what we're doing here," Agent Medina said with a warm smile.

Huh? Irma thought with just a smidge of disappointment.

"Mr. Lair told us about your little get-together this evening," Agent Medina said.

"And he was kind enough to invite us to dinner," Agent McTiennan finished.

"We're actually investigating the disappearance of a friend of yours," Agent Medina said with a note of apology in her voice.

She reached into the breast pocket of her blazer and pulled out a small, glossy photo of a girl.

The image jolted Irma out of her spy game and back to reality. She felt a lump rise in her throat.

We Guardians have more than portal-closing and world-saving on our to-do lists now, she thought. We also have to evade government agents who could do us some serious harm. They could even toss us in jail!

And, Irma thought gloomily, it's all because of the girl in that picture.

"Elyon!" Cornelia cried.

SIX

Cornelia felt light-headed as she realized exactly what was happening. In the dining room of her goofy friend, Irma, she was actually staring down two agents from Interpol!

Agent Medina—a sweet-faced woman hiding her pretty brown eyes behind big, round spectacles—oozed maternal warmth as she fanned some snapshots out on the white tablecloth. The first photo, the one that had made Cornelia gasp and cry out, was a picture Cornelia had taken of Elyon. Always a bit shy and giggly, Elyon had held her hand up to block the camera. Still, Cornelia had managed to capture her friend's face in midlaugh.

Beneath that first portrait was a snapshot of Elyon and Cornelia. They were posing on a park bench, looking at each other.

Wait a minute, Cornelia thought, as her breath started coming in short, shallow gasps. She looked wildly from the snapshots to her friends' faux grins to the agents' serious faces.

In order to find these photos, Cornelia realized, those agents must have searched Elyon's house! I wonder what *else* they found there.

She was thinking, of course, about the portal to Metamoor, located beneath Elyon's house in a secret, brick-lined tunnel. The Guardians had discovered the portal some time ago, but hadn't been able to close it.

And that was only because the brick walls came to life and attacked us, Cornelia thought in annoyance. It was either close the portal or escape with our lives. We chose the latter.

Shuddering at that horrible memory, Cornelia distracted herself with another look at the photos strewn on the tabletop and at her best friend's impish grin. She missed Elyon so much! Her shoulders slumped and she felt tears start to form in the corners of her eyes.

That was when Cornelia felt Irma at her side. She reached over and gave her a squeeze that said, "We're all here together."

Glancing at Irma gratefully, Cornelia straightened up. She hadn't realized it, but Agent Medina was speaking to her again.

"From the looks of it, you and Elyon were very close," she said.

"Yes, yes, we were," Cornelia said coldly. "What was your name again, Ms. . . ."

"Call me Maria," the woman said. She placed a small hand on her partner's broad shoulder. "And this is Joel. Our friends call us Big Guy and Small Fry."

"I can't imagine why," Joel said, laughing heartily.

Cornelia crossed her arms over her chest and gazed at the agents. She knew just what they were trying to do with their forced friendliness. They were trying to make Cornelia lower her guard.

Well, she thought with a disdainful sniff, obviously they don't know Cornelia Hale very well at all.

"Agent . . . Medina, right?" Cornelia said, archly refusing to use the woman's first name. "I'd prefer not to talk about this right now."

"Excuse me?" Agent Medina said, staring at Cornelia in surprise.

In reply, Cornelia merely pursed her thin lips and cast her gaze downward.

"There's no need to get defensive," Agent Medina said quickly. "We don't want to question you. We just—"

"Um!" Will interrupted from her seat next to Agent Medina's, trying to get the agent's attention. Once the woman turned to her, Will looked around wildly for a good reason to have interrupted. Cornelia saw her friend's eyes fall upon a jar of pickles resting next to her bread plate. She picked it up in her slightly trembling hand and handed it to Agent Medina.

"Could . . . you help me get this jar open?" she stuttered.

Nice save, Will, Cornelia thought.

Will always seemed a little shy and insecure, but in a pinch, she *always* managed to come up with a good solution. Cornelia couldn't help being impressed.

But Cornelia would have to wait to praise Will. Agent Medina was suspicious. She continued to stare Cornelia down as she took the jar from Will and gave the lid a twist.

"*Urgh,*" she grunted when the cap wouldn't budge. She tried again. Again, no luck. Finally, the agent peeled her gaze from Cornelia and frowned down at the jar, distracted.

At the same moment, Cornelia felt Irma grab her by the elbow and announce, "You know what? We need to get Cornelia some dry clothes. Coming, Corny?"

"Huh?" Cornelia said, a little confused. "Oh, yeah!"

She and Irma began to hurry out of the dining room. For added effect, Cornelia clapped a hand to her mouth and let forth a dramatic "ah-choo!"

"Hear that?" Irma cried out, giving Cornelia's arm a conspiratorial squeeze. "She's probably catching a cold. You go ahead and start without us."

As she followed Irma out of the room, Cornelia took one last glance at the dinner party. While she and Irma made a dash for it, Will was clearly going to keep up the evasive tactics in the dining room. She was smiling sweetly at Agent Medina, whose face was turning purple from the effort of prying off the stubborn lid.

"So . . ." Will drawled. "Mr. Lair says you're an expert in pedagogy, right?"

"Close," Agent Medina said, finally giving up on the pickle-jar lid. With a defeated sigh, she handed it to her partner. "I deal with criminal psychology."

"Oh, right!" Will said quickly. "And you, Mr. McTiennan? What do you deal with?"

Agent McTiennan watched Cornelia leave the room as he effortlessly popped open the pickle jar.

"I deal," he grumbled, "with everything else!"

Great, Cornelia thought as she and Irma rushed down the hallway to Irma's bedroom. Those nosy Interpol agents are acting even nosier.

As soon as the two girls were safe in her room, Irma sank onto the bed, her hands anxiously clasped together.

"Sorry, sorry, sorry!" she shrilled, almost as if responding to Cornelia's angry thoughts. "Dad brought them here without warning me."

Cornelia grabbed a towel that happened to be hanging off Irma's desk. She began squeezing the moisture out of her long hair.

"I just hope they haven't found the portal in Elyon's basement yet," she said.

The moment the words came out of her mouth, Cornelia's anger fired up.

What am I saying? She scolded herself. I'm magical. I shouldn't sit here passively *hoping* for results. I should create them!

Cornelia marched back to Irma's bedroom door and pushed it open a crack.

"Where are you going?" Irma whispered to Cornelia's back.

"Just investigating a bit," Cornelia replied, peeking down the hallway. She listened closely to see if she could hear any snatches of conversation coming from the dining room. Nothing. It was silent.

Something did catch her eye, however. It was a black briefcase sitting on a small table near the front door.

That's clearly government-issue pleather, Cornelia noted. She doubted Irma would have recognized such a subtle fashion detail. And here's another detail, Cornelia said to herself. There's something poking out of the bag.

"It looks like there's a file in that bag," Cornelia whispered over her shoulder to Irma.

"But that's Agent Medina's," Irma hissed. "Do you want to get into serious trouble?!"

"I just want to find out what those two know," Cornelia retorted. "I'll put everything back as soon as I'm done."

Before Irma could squeak out another protest, Cornelia tiptoed out of the bedroom. Using the grace she'd perfected in her skating lessons, Cornelia slunk down the hallway and plucked the file out of the briefcase. She dashed back to Irma's room, glancing back to see if anyone had spotted her. Irma slammed the door shut after her.

Quickly, Cornelia spread the file's contents out on Irma's pink bedspread.

"Look," she said breathlessly. "These are Elyon's drawings! She made these when she was little."

"Medina's a psychologist," Irma pointed out. "She must want to study them."

Cornelia sifted through the papers. Memories stabbed at her as she gazed at the crayoned drawings, all done in Elyon's precocious style. Cornelia wanted to cry, she missed her old friend so badly.

Just before she gave in to the tears, though, Cornelia shook her head.

I can't let my emotions get in the way, she

said to herself. I have a mystery to unravel. Speaking of which, here's a weird image. . . .

Cornelia had just happened upon a drawing at the bottom of the stack. In it, a little girl with wings and a long, blue gown was flying over a skyline of medieval buildings—from small cheery cottages to tall stone castles. The palaces were topped by turrets, ramparts, and strings of colorful flags. Elyon had clearly used all sixty-four colors in her crayon box to create the festive landscape.

But what about the flying girl? Cornelia wondered. She was wearing a glowing, golden crown upon her blond hair, but her face was nothing but a smudge, a mar caused by a drop of water or a tear.

I wonder what caused that tear to fall, Cornelia thought pensively. And perhaps even more interesting are those buildings! They look strangely familiar.

"Take a good, close look, Irma," Cornelia said, holding up the picture as Irma joined her at the bed. "Does this city remind you of anything?"

"Talking Turtles!" Irma cried after one glance. "It's Meridian!"

"So it's true," Cornelia breathed in astonishment. "Through her drawings, Elyon saw Metamoor, the place where she was born."

"You mean, she knew she wasn't from here?" Irma gasped.

"No," Cornelia insisted. "I think she drew those without realizing what she was doing."

That has to be the case, Cornelia added silently. If I'm wrong, that would mean Elyon was lying to me all those years. I won't believe that. I *can't* believe it!

Irma sank thoughtfully onto her bed. She studied the drawing carefully.

"But Metamoor's sad and gloomy," she said with a confused frown. "This place is bright and cheery!"

Cornelia got up and walked over to Irma's bedroom window to gaze out at the hard, gray rain and the gloom that reminded her of Metamoor.

"Maybe Elyon drew what the city of Meridian used to be like," she wondered aloud. "Maybe that's the Metamoor of the past."

"Or the Metamoor of the future," Irma proposed. She looked up from the drawing suddenly. "See this flying girl?" she asked.

Cornelia turned back to the bed, where Irma was pointing at the flying princess. Cornelia nodded.

"It looks like her face was smudged by a drop of water," Irma said. "But water is my element."

With a puff of blue magic sparkling at her fingertip, Irma tapped the spot. Cornelia peered over Irma's shoulder at the drawing.

"I can reconstruct the features of her face," Irma said dreamily. Using her index finger, she gently massaged her magic into the blurred drawing.

It was working! Slowly, the face was morphing from a smudge to a cloudy pair of eyes and a couple of hazy, pink spots.

"Soon we'll see. . . ." Irma whispered. She kept caressing the picture gently, lifting the damage away.

Finally, she raised her hand. Her magic dissipated with a little fizz.

Cornelia's eyes widened as she gazed at Elyon's drawing. The flying princess's face was clear now. Her eyes were blue and wide-set. The rosy cheeks were the same ones Elyon had always drawn in her childhood self-portraits.

The smile was broad, but shy.

So, it's true, Cornelia thought with a gasp of understanding. It is—it can only be—

Irma spoke the words for her.

"Elyon," she said softly. "The Light of Meridian."

SEVEN

Will woke up with a start. Her eyes flapped open.

That's weird, she thought woozily. I was just dreaming that someone was narrating my life, like a sports announcer following a soccer game. He started with me waking up. Then he went on to list all the things I'd been dreaming about—

She had been dreaming about Irma, Cornelia, Elyon, and—

Wait a minute, Will thought, her eyes opening even wider. Someone *is* narrating my life. And I know just who it is. . . .

"Alarm clock!" Will cried accusingly. She sat up and propped her chin on her hands, glaring irritably at the shelf behind her bed's headboard. Her alarm clock was, indeed, chattering away about Will's innermost thoughts in an annoying, nasal voice. Its red numbers flashed with every syllable.

Wow, Will thought as she rubbed the sleep from her eyes. Being magical is cool and all, but *this* power—being able to converse with all my electrical appliances—is taking some getting used to. All this magical stuff is strange . . . and getting stranger.

Like the power I discovered I possessed yesterday at Mr. Olsen's pet shop, Will thought. Who would believe that animals can sense my feelings! If I get cranky, they start meowing, howling, and yowling. If I cheer up, they purr. Worst of all, when I swooned over Matt at the shop yesterday, Pepe the parrot started squawking out my supersecret feelings.

Thinking about Matt made Will feel all gushy. She couldn't help it. Matt was her megacrush of all time. She would *die* if he found out how much she liked him, especially from a source as bizarre as an empathic, exotic bird!

It would also be highly humiliating, Will thought, if Matt ever learned of her *less* than loving feelings toward Jackie Gilligan. Jackie was older than Will, cooler than Will, and also happened to have the distinction of being Matt's crush.

Matt almost did find out just how I feel about Jackie, yesterday, Will thought, cringing. Once again it was that blabberbeak Pepe who almost spilled the beans.

It had happened when Matt's grandfather, Mr. Olsen—the sweet old man who owned the pet store where Will sometimes worked—had walked into the store with a slobbery Saint Bernard puppy. As the shaggy dog had snuffled his way around the shop, Mr. Olsen had explained to Matt and Will that he was dog-sitting while the puppy's owner was on vacation.

"Hey," Matt had exclaimed after a good look at the Saint Bernard. "That's Hefty, Jackie Gilligan's puppy!"

Will's couldn't help but pout.

Her mood had gone from happy to sad in mere seconds.

And every animal in the pet shop had responded with barks, meows, cheeps, and squeaks of anguish! It had been a total disaster.

If *Matt* had understood those animals' thoughts, Will thought with a shake of her head, he'd know that I've had a crush on him ever since the day we met.

I need to remember that Matt's the lead singer in a band, she thought. He falls for types like Jackie Gilligan, with her perfectly styled hair, her teensy-tiny skirts, and her long, white coat with the faux-fur trim. A white coat would get grubby and gross if I even just *looked* at it. I guess that's the difference between someone who could never get a guy like Matt Olsen and someone who could!

Will sighed. Crushing on Matt was blissfully excruciating. Or excruciatingly blissful. Will could never decide which. All she knew was—

Your dreams were crazy last night, Will. Must be all that rich food you ate at Irma's house.

Will was jolted out of her romantic ruminating by more prattling from her pesky alarm clock. She sat up in bed and glared at the appliance.

"How do you know what I ate?" she demanded of the clock. "And . . . what I dreamed about?"

You talk in your sleep, the clock said saucily. *And since I'm an alarm clock, I'm always too wired to doze off.*

That does it, Will thought. An alarm clock with attitude. I've really got to put a stop to this.

Will twisted around in her bed and gazed beyond the socks, slippers, half-read books, stuffed frogs, and other junk that littered her bedroom floor. Finally, her eyes came to rest upon her mother, who was standing in Will's doorway in her favorite robe and giving her daughter a stern look.

"M—Mom!" Will cried. "How long have you been there?"

"Long enough to know that you're talking to yourself," Mom said, planting a fist on one hip. Her voice was harsh and exhausted, even though the day had barely begun.

"Come on," she said briskly. "Breakfast is ready."

As her mom stalked off toward the kitchen, Will jumped out of bed and shoved her feet into her lime-green slippers.

I have to be more careful, she thought, scolding herself. If Mom found out I talk to electrical appliances, I don't know what she'd—

"Will!"

Mom's exasperated voice floated out of the loft's open kitchen to Will's bedroom. Will sighed and began to walk down the hall. Something told her this breakfast was *not* going to be the most fun meal of the day.

"I don't ask much of you," Mom began when Will arrived in the kitchen.

Oh, boy, Will sighed. Here comes the nagging.

"But you could do at least one thing," Mom said. "Just one. Is that too much to ask? And that thing is—your room! You have got to clean it up, and I want you to do it this morning."

"*This* morning?" Will said with a jokey smile as she plopped herself down at the breakfast table. Being playful with her mom always lightened the mood. "Like, right now? I mean, right away? I mean, right this *second*?"

Mom's face became fiery. Joking around was clearly not the way to go.

"Now!" she yelled impatiently. "As in, five minutes. Or ten! Just as long as you get it done. Got it?"

Will gasped softly, then looked away from

her mother. She felt anger and humiliation shoot through her like a spray of scalding water. She shoved her chair back with a loud scrape. Out of the corner of her eye, she saw her mom's hand fly to her mouth.

"I'm sorry, honey," Mom said, her voice suddenly wobbly and weak. "It's just that the house is a wreck, and I—"

"Have a nice breakfast," Will barked, refusing to meet her mother's eyes and unwilling to forgive.

A few well-broadcast stomps later, she was back in her room, slamming—and locking—the door behind her.

Mad, huh? the alarm clock chirped as Will stomped across the room. *Can I do anything?*

"Yeah!" Will snapped. "Snooze!"

Fine, the alarm clock retorted. *If that's your attitude, then I won't tell you that your cell phone rang.*

"Huh?" Will said. In midstomp, she stopped to look at the clock. "Really?"

Will did a quick scan of her room. She saw yesterday's homework, a couple of CDs, a stuffed frog, a pile of blue jeans, and her dormouse. The cell phone, however, was AWOL.

"Phone, phone, phone," Will grumbled, dropping to her knees in the middle of her room. She began tossing clothes, stuffed animals, and magazines over her shoulders as she burrowed around in the mess, looking for the elusive gadget. "Where did I put you?"

Hmph!

Will heard an indignant—and muffled—squeak. It was the voice of her cell phone! She'd have recognized it anywhere.

I'm down here, the phone grumbled from the bottom of the jeans pile. *Like, maybe you should listen to your mother every once in a while.*

"Would you mind your own business?" Will grumbled as she finally located the phone. She looked the phone right in the, er, screen and added, "Just tell me who called."

I didn't hear the magic word, it complained. *Did you hear the magic word, alarm clock?*

Across the room, the alarm clock said in a really obnoxious tone, *I'm snoozing.*

Will rolled her eyes.

"All right, already!" she finally sputtered. "Please!"

A moment later, Will was dialing Cornelia. As

she waited for her friend to answer, she began listlessly picking clothes up off the floor.

As long as my mother is *making* me clean my room, she thought, I might as well multitask.

Finally, Cornelia picked up. "Hi! I was waiting for you to call back!"

Will was glad her phone had come through in a pinch.

"I can't get in touch with the other girls," Cornelia said, sounding frustrated.

Hay Lin is talking to Irma, Will's gossip-loving cell phone informed Cornelia. *And Taranee is talking to Nigel.*

"How do you know that?" Cornelia gasped, mistaking the cell phone's voice for Will's.

"That was my nosy phone talking," Will explained.

Hey, I heard it through the phone-line grapevine, the phone piped up.

Cornelia didn't even laugh at the phone's quip. She must have been majorly distressed not to have a comment.

"Will!" she told her friend. "Those agents we met at Irma's are staked out at my house! I'm on my balcony and I can see them, parked right down the street from my building."

"What?" Will cried. She could picture Cornelia, scared and shivering as she gazed down at the agents' car from her window. "Do they think you had something to do with Elyon's disappearance?"

"I don't know," Cornelia said. "I must have made them suspicious last night. The minute I go outside, they'll start following me."

"Well . . . so what?" Will said. "You've got nothing to hide, right?"

"Today we're going to Elyon's house to close the portal in the basement," Cornelia reminded her.

"Right!" Will said, slapping her forehead. With all the mom-daughter drama going on in her own home, she'd completely forgotten about the Guardian drama awaiting her outside.

There's just way too much drama going on in general, Will complained silently. But she didn't have time to stress about that now. Her friend needed her.

"I'll come over and help you soon," Will promised Cornelia. "I just have to stop by the pet shop for a second and . . ."

Will scanned her room, which was still *far* from cleaned up.

". . . And do one other little thing," she sighed. "See you."

Ten minutes later, Will was standing in the middle of her clutter-free bedroom floor, gazing around the room. The bed was made. The rug was freshly swept. The stuffed frogs were all stashed on bookshelves, and the clothes had been tossed into the closet.

There we go! Will thought with a small smile of satisfaction. My room is spotless. Mom *can't* have anything else to say.

Knock, knock, knock.

"Will? There's something I have to tell you."

My mistake, Will sighed. She *does* have more to say.

"Actually," Mom continued, her voice muffled as she spoke from behind the door, "I should have told you last night, but you were at Irma's and—"

"And you were at Mr. Collins's," Will retorted. "So I'd say we're even."

"Dean was helping me with an important decision," Mom continued.

Yeah! Will thought, flopping onto her bed with a scowl. I bet!

"Please . . . Will," Mom said, choking up.

Will's scowl softened.

It sounded as if her mom were crying.

Maybe I'd better not push it, Will thought. She heaved herself off the bed.

"I'll open up," she called to her mother as she walked to the door. "But I'm telling you right now, I'd love it if we could talk minus all the tears."

Will stood back as she turned the knob. She was bracing herself for her mother's big entrance—when something distracted her. She saw a flash of blue at her window. Twisting around for a better look, Will almost screamed.

Actually, there was a whole *lot* of blue in her window. The window frame strained to contain the torso of a giant monster with cobalt-colored skin, hands the size of hams, and beady—but kind—eyes.

"Vathek!" Will gasped in recognition.

Talk about an entrance, she thought in a panic. There's no way I can let Mom see him!

"Bath . . . what?" Mom stuttered. She was already halfway through the door.

Will stifled another scream. She bit her lip and spun around, looking for a solution.

She could come up with only one.

Cringing with regret, Will slammed the bedroom door in her mother's face.

EIGHT

Vathek grunted as he hoisted himself up a tree, straining toward Will's window.

Why, he wondered in exasperation, does the Keeper of the Heart of Candracar want to live so high up in the air?

Vathek wobbled dangerously as he moved from branch to branch.

"And these earth trees," he moaned. "They're so spindly. They would barely heat my house in Metamoor for an hour. Not that I ever need to worry about that sort of thing again."

Ever since Vathek had betrayed his master, Cedric, and joined Metamoor's rebels, he'd had to steer clear of his home. He was Prince Phobos's enemy now, and therefore, an exile and a wanted beast.

Vathek hung his big, blue head at the thought. Part of him still couldn't believe he'd done something so noble. It was the first time, really, that he'd *ever* thought for himself. It had been terrifying. And he had ended up all alone—for a while.

He was tremendously relieved to have a new master to serve now.

Actually, Vathek corrected himself as he continued his climb, make that *mistress*! Young Elyon. The queen-to-be is so tiny, yet so powerful. It's hard to believe she once lived among these girls.

Vathek finally reached the window of the Guardian named Will and peeked through it.

What a mess! Vathek thought with wide eyes. Inside her room, Will was scurrying around, scooping up garments and tossing them irritably into a closet.

Why pick clothes up off the bedroom floor, only to throw them onto the closet floor? Vathek wondered, scratching his leathery forehead with a claw.

As Vathek pondered that mystery, Will finished her cleaning. Then she began talking to her bedroom door.

Well, now, that is strange, too, Vathek thought. Perhaps talking to doors is another earth custom I don't understand.

Vathek began to haul himself through the window. It was a tight fit and a noisy one, too. He'd distracted the young Guardian from her conversation with the door.

"Vathek!" she cried.

"Did I pick a bad time, Guardian?" Vathek inquired as he finished climbing through the window and tumbled onto the floor.

Will leaned heavily against the door and scowled at Vathek.

"You picked a bad time, bad place, and bad entrance," she hissed. "You big ape!"

"Hey!" the door suddenly piped up. "Will, is this your idea of a joke or of a punishment?"

"My, I've never known wood to be so surly," Vathek said, gaping at the disagreeable door.

"I thought I could talk with you calmly and maturely, but I guess I was wrong!" the door continued.

Will pressed both hands against the door and glanced back at Vathek with wide brown eyes.

"What do I do?" she muttered under her

breath. "What do I do, what do I do?"

Vathek shrugged. He honestly had no experience with talking a door down from rage. The Guardian was on her own.

Or was she?

The door was beginning to move, and so was Will—right toward Vathek!

The door spoke again.

"Get ready to listen," it said, "because I'm coming in!"

Will gasped. With a wild look in her eyes, she dived across the room and began ripping the sheets off her sleigh-shaped bed.

"What are you do—" Vathek began to ask.

Then, everything went black.

By the Light of Meridian, he wondered in panic, what has become of me? Has the Guardian used magic to plunge me into a wormhole? Maybe she's made me blind! Oh, wait. My eyes were closed. . . .

Vathek opened his eyes and saw . . . a giant frog. It was woven into a blanket of some sort, which had been thrown over his head. Slivers of light crept in through the thin fabric.

That wasn't all he saw. His meaty left arm was draped in a pink quilt. His right had a rug thrown over it. A lavender sheet was wrapped around his belly, and the weight on the back of his neck felt like a ruffly pillow.

He was about to rip all the coverings away when he heard the door speak again. This time, its voice sounded closer. It must have lifted itself off its hinges and walked right in!

Fascinated, Vathek cocked his heavy head to listen.

"Wow," the door said with a sarcastic edge in its voice. "I see you've been working hard."

"Yeah!" Will stuttered nervously. "That is, no! Um, I mean, I still have to put a few things in their places, here and there."

"So, I see we've stooped to playing tricks!"

As the door addressed Will, Vathek spotted a triangle of light through his draperies. A peephole! He shifted his head until he could see through it.

Oh! He thought. It's a woman.

Vathek watched the woman toss her long, glossy, black hair and fold her arms as she berated the young Guardian.

"Fine!" she yelled. "I have to go now. We'll talk later, when you've decided to grow up!"

The woman turned on her heel and stormed

off, slamming the door behind her.

Vathek heard Will emit a big sigh.

Feeling a twinge of regret for barging in with no warning, Vathek pulled the froggy covering off his head.

"Is she gone?" he said to the disgruntled Guardian in front of him.

"Yeah, but I think her face was even bluer than yours!" Will said, glaring up at Vathek. "What are you doing here? Shouldn't you be in Metamoor?"

Vathek took a deep breath. Here it was—the reason for his mission.

"Guardian!" he intoned importantly. "I come with a plea for help—from Elyon!"

At Will's bewildered stare, Vathek puffed out his chest to begin his tale.

"Elyon came to see us—that is, me and the other rebels," he began. "She came late at night, hiding beneath the hood of a brown cloak. To reach us, she put her own life at risk and braved the underground world of the endless city."

Vathek remembered the scene clearly. Two armed guards had brought Elyon to him. He'd assumed she was looking for Caleb, the young—and handsome—leader of the rebels.

"Caleb isn't here," he'd declared to the girl as she stood before the table where Vathek had been drinking from a tankard of cider. "He's out recruiting rebels in your name."

"I'm here for help, Vathek," Elyon had replied calmly. "You have to help me free my adoptive parents."

Stunned, Vathek had stood up. He'd stepped closer to Elyon and gazed down at her sympathetically.

"I know that I disowned them," Elyon had said with a quiver in her thin voice. "But I've also seen where they're being kept. It's a horrible place."

"The prison is a creation of your brother's," Vathek had explained. "They lock up anyone who thinks differently from him."

"They're suffering! I can feel it," Elyon had gasped. She'd thrown back her hood to reveal her face. It was pinched and pale. Her liquid eyes were filled with anguish. "They'll never survive until my coronation."

Vathek did not want to deny her, but he'd had to.

"No one can break into the prison, not even

I!" he'd said. "You should ask the Guardians for help."

"No!" Elyon cried shrilly. "Except for Cornelia, they all hate me. They won't help me."

"Hmmm," Vathek had said, putting a claw to his craggy chin. "I'm not exactly a genius, but it's easy to see that if you've come all the way here, eluding Phobos's control, it means that you might be doubting him. Perhaps the moment has come for you to believe in someone else, Light of Meridian!"

Vathek emerged from his story to refocus on Will.

"And so," he continued somberly, "Elyon chose you, the Guardians of the Veil, to believe in—to help her."

Will frowned at him. Then she frowned at the floor, deep in thought. As she deliberated, she began to burrow into her closet. She pulled out an assortment of garments. Vathek spotted a straw hat with a pink ribbon, a red feather boa, and a frilly, blue scarf.

Will's expression was shifting from ponderous to mischievous. She began walking toward him, holding the goofy garments out in front of her.

"Guardian," Vathek grunted. "You're not thinking, you don't mean . . . No, Guardian!"

Within five minutes, the red-haired girl had dressed Vathek in girlish frippery. She'd even topped the ensemble off with a fur-trimmed coat!

After that, she'd led him out to the street.

The pair began to walk through the city. Each human being they passed gazed in astonishment at Vathek's giant, blue form in its colorful clothes.

Will took no notice. She was too busy questioning Vathek.

"Okay," she said as she stomped down the sidewalk, her hands thrust deep into the pockets of her orange vest. "Let's imagine for a minute that your story about Elyon is true. Why did you come to me, Vathek?"

"I've always found it difficult," Vathek began, "to get my bearings in your confusing city—"

"Heatherfield isn't *my* city," Will said crossly. "And unlike yours, it's pretty easy to get around in."

"Anyway," Vathek said, wondering why the

girl was so grumpy, "I could only remember how to get to your place. Back when I worked for Cedric, he kept a watchful eye on you."

Will gave Vathek a sidelong and suspicious glance.

"I can't imagine how you managed to hide when you worked for him!" she declared, eyeing his blue skin.

"Well, *he* was a master of deception," Vathek hurled back. "We didn't need to rely on silly costumes."

"Hey," Will retorted. "These clothes were all I could find, okay?"

"People are staring at me," Vathek complained as he and the girl tromped down the sidewalk. "When I got here earlier, no one was around."

"That's because it was raining," Will said. "We have to find a way to get to Cornelia's without drawing too much attention."

Will walked in silence for a moment.

There she goes again, Vathek thought, as Will became lost in thought.

"I've got it!" Will suddenly declared. "Matt's grandfather's van! We'll kill two birds with one stone!"

Oh, my, Vathek thought, pushing the tickly feather boa away from his chin. I have *no* idea what that means. I just want to know one thing. . . .

"Do you plan to disguise me," he asked Will, "as a bird or a stone?"

"Very funny, Vathek," Will said as she stepped up her pace.

With the monster in tow, Will crossed several more streets, each one full of smoke-spewing vehicles. Vathek sighed in relief when they reached a small, boxy building. Will sneaked Vathek into a walled lot behind it. The sandy ground was littered with large metal canisters that smelled like rotten food. There were boxes, too, and a long, bulbous-looking vehicle. Large letters in bubble type on the vehicle's side read: *Olsen's Pet Shop.*

"And you intend to use this contraption?" Vathek asked of Will.

"I don't think we have any alternative," Will answered him. "Now, for the final touch."

Will stood tall and held out her fist. Wisps of pink magic began creeping out from between her clenched fingers. When she opened her hand, the Heart of Candracar was floating above her palm. Its crystal orb glowed and throbbed. Rays of light shot from the Heart, and billows of smoke rose up around Will's feet. From one of those puffs of steam, a figure emerged! It was a man with thin, white hair, wire-rimmed spectacles, and a sweet grin.

Oh, Vathek thought in disappointment. He was expecting something a little more dramatic.

"With all the spells in your power," he demanded of the Guardian, "you couldn't create anything but an old man?"

"It's a double of Matt's grandfather," Will explained. "We call them astral drops. He knows everything the real man knows—which means he can drive!"

Will turned her back on Vathek and muttered to herself, "At least I hope so! Whenever I create an astral drop, I always goof something up."

What? Vathek thought in alarm. He opened his mouth to voice his protest when, suddenly, the astral grandfather interrupted him.

"Hello, there, pretty lady!" he said. He batted his white eyelashes as he gazed at Vathek's fur coat and fluffy boa.

"Guardian!" Vathek roared. Now he was *really* alarmed.

Will, of course, was merely amused.

"Um, wait for me in the van," she said to Vathek and Astral Mr. Olsen, with a giggle in her voice. "I'll feed the animals and be right back."

Vathek looked incredulously from the impudent earth girl to the flirty astral drop.

And I thought I was confused by this mad planet before, he thought. I have a feeling things are only going to get crazier.

NINE

Will looked at the astral drop of Matt's grand-father. As Astral Mr. Olsen smoothed his white hair and straightened his scarf, Will felt a bit queasy.

You'd think I wouldn't be so weirded out by this magical double, she mused. It's not like I haven't dealt with astral drops before. One time when I went to Metamoor, I had to create a double of myself to take my place. Now, *that* was weird. I watched that alternate Will walk like me and talk like me and ride my bike off to my home to impersonate me. . . .

Will cringed as she thought about what had happened next. As it turned out, the astral version of Will had been a bit flawed.

Okay, Will thought as she chuckled. A *lot* flawed. In fact, she was dumb as a post. She barely knew my address!

A second hard look at Astral Mr. Olsen confirmed that he, too, might have been short a few marbles.

"This is a pretty nice joint," he was saying to the horrified Vathek. He gazed around the pet store's cluttered backyard as if it were a happening nightspot. "You come here often?"

Will slapped her forehead.

What am I doing? she thought. I clearly have astral-drop issues. Well, let's just hope Mr. Olsen can do what I conjured him up to do and drive that van! I guess I'll find out right after I finish this chore.

Will turned away from the magical man and the Metamoorian monster and hurried to the pet shop's back door. Her daunting to-do list was buzzing around in her mind, making her slightly dizzy.

I'll have to figure out a way to help Cornelia, she thought, pulling out her key. And I have to get the other girls together and—

Will's thoughts halted as she unlocked the door and stepped inside the quiet store. Her breathing seemed to stop, too. Make that, her entire life! Everything ground to an abrupt halt as Will found herself staring at the slightly disheveled, but totally cute, back of Matt Olsen!

"Eeek!" Will shrieked. "Matt!"

"Aaagh!" Matt cried. He'd been leaning over an aquarium when Will barged in. Now, he spun around, spilling fish food all over the floor. "Will!"

On the one hand, Will totally couldn't deal with seeing Matt right now. On the other, she was elated at seeing him. She was *so* elated that she could barely stutter out a hello.

"S—sorry," she finally blurted out, stepping toward her crush with a goofy grin on her face. "I didn't think I'd see you here. Don't you have band practice or something?"

"The drummer's sick," Matt said, smiling back at Will. He ducked his head shyly, loping over to check on a box of kittens under one of the counters. "So I thought I'd just feed the animals," he said, leaning down to pet a kitten.

"I was supposed to do that," Will said.

"Well, yeah. I mean . . . I knew that," Matt said. He stood up and looked at Will in a way he'd never done before. He seemed nervous and excited and cocky and insecure, all at once. "That's why I stopped by, actually."

That did it. Will stopped breathing once again. In a second, she was going to turn blue!

"I was just wondering," Matt continued, casting his gaze downward. "Are you free tonight?"

Will's ability to breathe returned with a quiet gasp. Could this be? Was Matt Olsen actually, really, truly asking her out?

To her dismay, the very worst question popped out of Will's mouth.

"Huh? Are you kidding?" she said. She couldn't believe how hard she was grinning or how hot her face felt.

My cheeks are bright red, Will thought, and probably glowing like holiday lights. But who cares? Matt wants to go out with me.

"Of course, I'm . . ." she started to say.

Suddenly, Will felt her giddiness fizzle. She couldn't *believe* what she had to say next!

". . . Not!" Will said sadly. "Well, actually, maybe I am. That is, um, it depends."

In her head, Will groaned.

What can I say? she thought desperately.

Oh, I might be able to go out with you, Matt. But, first, I have to run a quick errand to another world. That sounds just great!

She had no good excuse.

Matt seemed equally confused.

"Yes, no, maybe, it depends," he said, his eyes becoming heavy-lidded with hurt. "You're always so mysterious. I . . . huh?"

Matt's attention had suddenly wandered—to the old man hanging out in the backyard.

"That's my grandfather!" Matt said in surprise. "He said he wouldn't be by until later."

I thought this moment couldn't get any worse, Will thought in a panic. *I should have known better!*

"Actually," she piped up nervously, "that's because of me! We have an errand to run. Yeah! We have to . . . um . . . to get . . . um . . ."

A million bad excuses later, Will had finally escaped the pet shop—and Matt's confused brown eyes.

She slumped into the passenger seat of the van. Vathek was already huddled in the back, hiding from the old man's gaze. Astral

Mr. Olsen was behind the wheel, fiddling with the dashboard controls in bemusement.

"Just be able to drive, Mr. Olsen," Will said with a soft sigh. "Please, let one thing work out. Be able to drive."

Screeeeech!

The van peeled out of the parking lot. Will clutched her door handle for support.

Well, I guess I didn't ask for him to drive *well*, Will thought with a little giggle.

She spent the next several minutes giving Astral Mr. Olsen directions to Cornelia's house. It was a welcome distraction from the thoughts pounding in her head—thoughts like: The first time I met Matt, I bonked him on the foot. Then Astral Will kissed him and slapped him. Now I've turned him down for a date.

My chances with this guy? They're now officially blown!

Will didn't really stop brooding until the van screeched to a halt in front of Cornelia's apartment building. Will took a deep breath and looked around. A plain black sedan was parked directly across the street, and sitting in the front seat were the unmistakable silhouettes of Agents Medina and McTiennan. They looked as if they were arguing.

Arguing about Cornelia, most likely, Will thought. Look at how they keep glancing up at her apartment building. Well, Agents, here's a nasty surprise for you. A few minutes from now, Cornelia's going to be nowhere near home.

Giving Astral Mr. Olsen a pointed look, Will flipped open her cell phone and began to dial Cornelia.

Two minutes later, Will's plan was in place. Following her instructions, Astral Mr. Olsen had wandered over to the Interpol agents' car and peeked into their window with a sweet and innocent grin.

"Hi, there," he said, just as she'd told him to. "Do you think you could tell me what that pedal is used for? The one on the left. . . ."

Meanwhile, Will hid behind the van. Peeking around its back door, which was open, she saw Agent McTiennan's face as Astral Mr. Olsen chattered away. The rock-jawed agent began pointing at his car's pedals and talking to Astral Mr. Olsen in obvious exasperation.

Good! Will thought happily. Whirling around, she signaled to the person who was standing behind the glass door at the front of Cornelia's building.

Immediately, Cornelia darted out. She was wearing a dark cap over her blond hair, and muted brown pants.

She rushed over and ducked behind the van with Will. As soon as she arrived, Will peeked at the agents again. They were still explaining the nuances of the clutch pedal to Astral Mr. Olsen. Perfect!

"What's going on?" Cornelia whispered to Will.

"Don't ask," Will replied, rolling her eyes. "Just get in the van!"

TEN

Heeding the urgency in Will's brown eyes, Cornelia clambered into the back of the van. Will slammed the doors shut with a jarring clank. Now Cornelia sat in the dark. Only a sliver of light shone through the window separating the front seat of the van from the back.

As Cornelia's eyes adjusted to the gloom, she could see that the pet-shop van looked as rickety as it sounded. It was lined with dilapidated, but clean, animal cages. Its floor had been stripped of carpeting, and it smelled stale and old.

But none of that was as remarkable as the thing in the corner!

"Vathek?" she breathed. The monster was curled up next to a pile of blankets, wearing a

voluminous fur coat and—a feather boa? "Uh, what are you wearing?"

"I don't want to talk about it," the giant Metamoorian creature said, irritably blowing an errant feather off his chin.

"O-kay," Cornelia said. Up front, she heard both van doors opening. Will climbed through the passenger-side door and sat low in her seat.

On the driver's side . . .

"Mr. Olsen? The pet-store owner?" Cornelia said in confusion. The whole scene just kept getting odder and odder.

The old man didn't answer Cornelia. He was too busy waving at someone across the street. Cornelia pressed her face to the little window in the side of the van for a peek.

What? she thought. Mr. Olsen is playing nice with my stalkers, those meddling Interpol agents!

"Well, thanks again," Mr. Olsen was saying. "I'll start following your suggestions right away."

Cornelia was officially confused. She was about to say as much to Will when the van suddenly lurched backward.

"Whoooooaaa!" Cornelia screamed.

"Wait a minute!" Will yelled at Mr. Olsen. "You're driving backward!"

What is going on? Cornelia thought in bewilderment.

A moment later, all thoughts faded from her mind completely. Mr. Olsen had screeched to a sudden stop. Then he jolted the van out of reverse and peeled forward.

The van shot away so fast that the back doors flew open.

"Aaargh!" Vathek cried. He grabbed at a couple of animal cages, trying to get a grip.

Cornelia was less scared of tumbling from the van than of being spotted by Agents Medina and McTiennan. Without thinking, she bolted toward the back of the van. Bracing her feet against two rough spots on the vehicle's metal floor, she reached out for the flapping doors.

"Got 'em!" she cried, as her long fingers closed around the door handles. "Yes!"

Just before Cornelia could swing the doors shut, though, she glanced up.

"No!" she cried.

She found herself staring straight into the outraged eyes of Agents Medina and

McTiennan. They had spotted her!

Just before Cornelia slammed the doors closed, she saw something else outside the van. Something that might save her!

Cornelia collapsed onto the floor, breathing hard. She closed her eyes and concentrated.

A moment later, Cornelia got up and clambered to the front of the van. Along the way, she shot Vathek a secret smile.

He responded with a bewildered grunt.

Ah, she thought smugly. Vathek's probably wondering what I have to be so happy about. Well, I'm simply imagining the conversation those two Interpol agents must be having at this moment.

"Now we know," Agent Medina would be blustering. "That old man wasn't clueless. He was trying to distract us! Look, the back of his van's just opened, and Cornelia's inside!"

Oh, yes, she is! Cornelia thought.

She returned to the imaginary scene in her head. McTiennan would be reaching for the car key by now, and turning it decisively. Instead of the roar of an engine catching, though, he'd be hearing the limp *vrrrrr, vrrrr, vrrrrrr* of an engine stalling.

"What are you waiting for?" Medina would be screeching at her partner now. "Follow them!"

"I'm trying!" McTiennan would grunt. "I'm trying!"

After a few more failed attempts to start the car, McTiennan would get out of the car and storm onto the sidewalk, yelling, "Nothing's happening. The car won't start! I have to open the hood."

Cornelia then imagined Medina leaning out of the car window to talk to McTiennan as he lifted the car's hood and peered at the engine.

"McTiennan," the smaller agent would say, "did you notice anything bizarre inside that van? I mean, apart from the old guy, who was clearly off his rocker?"

"I could have sworn I saw some sort of strange giant in the back with the girl," McTiennan would reply as he looked at what was under the hood. Then his eyes would grow wide as he looked at the engine that was now overgrown with shrubbery. He'd cry, "Do you think that's strange? This is plain ridiculous!"

No, Cornelia thought then, with a little giggle. That's what I like to call magic!

Feeling pretty good about her magical stunt, Cornelia smiled to herself as the van traveled away from her apartment building. The agents were a distant memory, too. Cornelia's engine plan had worked!

In the front seat, Will looked surprised to have shaken the meddlers so easily.

"What happened?" Will asked.

"Oh," Cornelia said coyly. She perched her pointy chin on the ledge of the back-to-front window and grinned. "I spotted a little plant sprouting from the asphalt beneath the agents' car. I just helped it grow—around the carburetor, the starter valve, and a few other crucial bits of the engine!"

"Whoo-hoo!" Will exclaimed. She held out her hand for a high five. Through the little window, Cornelia slapped her friend's palm. Independent as she was, she had to admit it *was* pretty fun being part of this crazy crew.

Even if we *are* a little odd, Cornelia thought, glancing from the big, blue creature to the old man, who was speeding them all down the road.

"Will," she said as Astral Mr. Olsen drove on, "you still haven't told me what Vathek and

Matt's grandfather are doing here."

"I'll explain it all later," Will said. "I just managed to contact the other girls. The group meeting at Elyon's house is still on!"

Cornelia felt another rush of adrenaline. There seemed to be more at stake here than just closing the portal. What was Will up to?

ELEVEN

Soon after Will, Cornelia, and Vathek had joined Irma, Taranee, and Hay Lin at Elyon's house, the whole group descended into the basement. From there, they entered a long, brick tunnel decorated with Gothic arches and dim, industrial-style lamps.

At the end of that tunnel was a portal to Metamoor.

Taranee heaved a deep breath as she contemplated the hole in the Veil. It was a roiling, round gash, shooting off sparks of magic in every direction.

We need just one thing, she thought, to face that kind of magic: even *more* magic!

Will seemed to be thinking the exact same thing.

As the young leader motioned for her friends to gather around her, Taranee felt a surge of warmth and strength. She and Will had had this bond—a silent communication—ever since they were newbies together at Sheffield.

Taranee wished she could whisper some words of encouragement in Will's ear, but there was no time. Will was doing her Heart of Candracar thing. The redheaded girl closed her eyes, held out her fist, and began the transformation.

First, Will's fist trembled and shook. Rays of hot pink magic broke through the spaces between her fingers. When she opened her hand, the Heart of Candracar, pulsing with energy, hovered above her palm.

Will thrust the orb toward Cornelia.

"Cornelia!" she cried. "Earth!"

A bobbling teardrop of energy shot toward the tallest Guardian. It whirled around her, trailing a cyclone of green magic in its wake.

"Irma!" Will shouted, turning now to the group's water girl. Quickly, Irma's jeans and sweater were replaced by turquoise and purple leggings, a miniskirt, and wings.

"Air!" Will continued, sending a silver teardrop of magic to Hay Lin.

Finally, she turned to Taranee.

"And, for you," she said, "fire!"

Taranee nodded and braced herself for her infusion of orange magic. Its power hit her like, well, like a bolt of fire! Taranee felt heat begin to pulse into her chest. From there, the magic traveled through her limbs. Her muscles contracted, absorbing new strength. Her bones lengthened, and her hair wound itself into wild, ribbonlike tendrils. Most thrillingly, she could feel wings unfurl from her back. Finally, Taranee's transformation was complete. She blinked herself out of her trancelike state, then gazed at her friends. It never ceased to amaze her how incredible they all looked.

I feel pretty incredible, too, Taranee admitted to herself shyly. I guess I've come a long way since the time when being magical made me want to hide under my bed and never come out.

It was true. After Taranee had conjured up her first fireball, she'd stayed up all night, afraid that she'd set her house on fire if she let herself dream. At school, she'd felt more shy and freakish than ever—until she'd realized that she wasn't alone in the magic-mission thing. Her fellow Guardians were powerful, too, after all. They were also true friends. With their help, Taranee had become more confident than she'd ever been.

I guess hanging out with Nigel didn't hurt, either, Taranee thought, glowing at the thought of her brown-haired crush.

Taranee sighed. She would have loved to lapse into a daydream about that boy right then and there.

Unfortunately, Will had already said something that Irma didn't agree with.

"No!" Irma was insisting loudly. "Going to Metamoor sounds like a horrible idea to me. I don't trust Vathek. What if he's serving Cedric again?"

"Irma's right," Hay Lin said, her face showing skepticism. "This could be a giant trap."

Hay Lin's probably remembering what it felt like the last time we were there, Taranee thought sympathetically, when she literally *was* trapped behind a brick wall.

Hay Lin continued.

"Vathek won't even tell us where we can

find the portal he used in order to get to Heatherfield," she complained.

"He doesn't know his way around the city," Will explained with a shrug. "And even if he knew where it was, he might have a hard time telling us how to get there, because—"

Aah-chooo!

Vathek had just interrupted Will with a bellowing, otherworldly sneeze.

"Uh, he's caught a strange cold," Will said with a giggle in her voice.

Cornelia, as usual, stood in direct opposition to Irma.

"I think we're all here," she declared. She pointed into the long, gloomy tunnel. "Down there, the portal's open. And if Vathek's story about Elyon's parents *is* true, we need to get moving—now!"

Taranee glanced at Will, who nodded.

Looks like we're taking another little trip to Metamoor, Taranee thought.

A few minutes later, the Guardians and Vathek arrived in Metamoor. They found themselves in a long corridor, deep beneath the streets of Metamoor's capital, Meridian.

Vathek—who had been flummoxed by the streets and intersections of Heatherfield—knew these Metamoorian passageways by heart. He grabbed a torch, which Taranee promptly lit with her fingertip. Then he began leading the girls through the underground labyrinth.

Everything was going smoothly. There was only one problem.

Ah-chooooo!

Vathek couldn't stop sneezing! With each of his bellowing explosions, the floor shifted beneath the Guardians' feet, the air rumbled, and dust filtered down from the ceiling onto the girls' hair.

The quakes made the Guardians nervous, but, even worse, they thoroughly exhausted the big, blue creature.

Finally, he'd sneezed his last sneeze.

"I can't go eddy furder dan dis, Guardiads," he declared with a wet sniff.

"That's okay, Vathek," Will quipped. "You'd probably draw the attention of Phobos's entire army with those sneezes, anyway."

Wiping his stubby nose with a claw, Vathek nodded. He crouched purposefully on the ground and began using the same claw to scratch a picture into the dirt. When Taranee leaned in to look, she saw it was a map.

"Wow," she gasped as the map took shape. "There's quite a maze of tunnels down here."

"Yeah, and I bet it's full of bugs," Irma said. She glanced into a dank corner with a shudder. "We could be wandering around down here for days!"

Cornelia squinted at the map. "I don't think so, Irma," she declared. "Look. Right now, we're seven stories underground—directly below the prison. And remember, earth . . ."

Cornelia stood up with gleam in her eyes.

". . . Is my element!"

Cornelia threw her arm into the air, and a geyser of green magic shot up over her head.

Ftoooom!

Cornelia's strike broke through the ceiling with a mighty *boom*. A moment later, the Guardians found themselves blinking up at a smoking hole.

"Ibpressive," Vathek said with another loud gurgly snort.

"Great job, Cornelia!" Will echoed. "Now, all we have to do is find a way to get up there and find Elyon's parents!"

With the help of Hay Lin's flying power, the
Guardians soon made it up to the next level of
the prison. The moment they arrived, however,
Taranee felt the urge to flee. The place was
awful—an endless corridor of tiny nooks
carved out of damp, moldy rock.

I thought the tower where Elyon locked *me*
up was bad, Taranee thought. That was a
palace compared to this joint.

Taranee and her friends ducked behind a
craggy corner in the stone wall to try to come
up with a plan.

"How will we find them?" Taranee whispered to the other Guardians as she peeked
back out at the cells. Bedraggled Metamoorians
cowered inside each one. The prisoners had
green or blue skin, jagged teeth, clawed feet,
and tails. "Surely, Elyon's parents are in their
nonhuman forms. We'll never recognize them!"

"True," Will whispered back. "But I think
we have somebody who can lead us to them!"

She pointed over Taranee's shoulder.

Taranee and the others spun around, then
stifled gasps as they saw their old nemesis—
Cedric, the snake-man. He was talking to one

of the pig-nosed prison guards.

The Guardians shrank farther into the shadows and craned their necks to listen in.

"I beg your pardon, my lord?" the guard was saying to Cedric, his head bowed.

"You heard me," Cedric declared, pointing to a dreary little cave about halfway down the aisle. "Open that cell and let the prisoners out."

Why would he do that? Taranee wondered. Is that Elyon's parents' cage? Has Cedric had a change of heart?

There was no time to ponder the question any further. Cedric had turned his attention toward a craggy wooden stake poking out of a nearby wall.

"That lever!" Cedric shouted at the guard. "Does it control the opening to the scuttler's cage?"

Scuttler? Taranee thought with a raised eyebrow. That sounds icky.

"Huh?" the guard said. "Uh, yes, my lord. But it's better not to touch it. That monster hasn't eaten yet."

Now Taranee felt her stomach lurch. This sounded a lot worse than icky.

"Poor creature," Cedric cooed. "Well, we

should see that he gets fed right away."

Scrick!

Cedric reached out and yanked the lever down. Then he slithered farther down the hall.

Tlank!

The door of the tiny cell began to open. Hearing cries of surprise from inside the cell, Taranee craned her neck to listen.

"Thomas!" a sweet, high-pitched voice cried. "The door! Someone's opened it!"

"Stay close, Eleanor," ordered a lower voice.

Thomas and Eleanor! Taranee thought with elation. Those are Elyon's parents' names! We found them!

The Guardians, however, had to stay hidden until the coast was clear. So they remained silent while the couple sampled their first taste of freedom. When they peeked out of their cell, Taranee saw that her hunch had been right. The wide-eyed couple had green skin and lizardlike claws. Eleanor had long, blue hair, and Thomas had forest-colored stripes on his cheeks. It would have been difficult to pick them out if they hadn't spoken.

"Well?" Eleanor said to her husband as she watched him survey the scene.

Taranee followed the man's gaze through the tunnel. Wait a minute, she thought. Cedric and that guard have completely disappeared!

"I don't understand," Mr. Brown said, echoing Taranee's thoughts. "Where are Cedric and—"

Skriiieeeek!

Taranee cried out and slapped her hands over her ears. The screeching was awful.

A moment later, she saw the creature that had created the sound. It was a cockroach the size of a house. The angry monster had just lunged around a corner in the passageway. It was heading straight toward the Browns' cell! And it looked angry!

"May the Light protect us!" Thomas screamed. "They've let loose a scuttler!"

The monster, ignoring the man's terror, turned toward the woman. It lifted one of its six-foot-long front legs and hit Eleanor, sending her flying down the corridor.

"Eleanor!" Thomas screamed.

"See what I mean?" Irma declared. "I told you this place was full of bugs!"

The Guardians didn't need to see any more. They stormed out of their hiding place and rushed to the Browns' aid. Taranee actually felt exhilarated as she ran, forming fireballs in each hand. As Thomas rushed to his wife's side— and away from the horrible scuttler—the Guardians formed a circle around the creature.

Hay Lin took the first shot at it.

"Stay back, you big roach!" she yelled, shooting a blast of wind into the bug's face.

"Good job, Hay Lin," Irma said. "Give him some air. Maybe he'll catch pneumonia."

Now it's time for my fireballs, Taranee thought. She was just rearing back for a baseball-style pitch when another burst of magic surprised her.

This time, it was a blast of pink light from the Heart of Candracar. Taranee stopped to look at Will. Strangely, Will seemed as surprised as any of the girls to see the Heart floating over her palm.

"Hey," she exclaimed. "This must be one tough monster. The Heart of Candracar is coming to the rescue!"

"Eleanor!" Thomas cried from behind the Guardians. "It's them—the Guardians of the Veil!"

As if to prove Will's point, the Heart suddenly erupted, shooting off a great burst of magic.

"Aaagh!" Taranee cried, shielding her eyes from the light. When it had subsided, she quickly blinked away the spots that had formed behind her lids.

Then she blinked harder! The mutant bug was nowhere to be seen.

"Huh?" Will said. "Where did it go?"

Skreek.

Incredulously, Taranee and her friends looked down. The formerly huge insect had shrunk to the size of a quarter! Now the squishable little squirt was fleeing across the stone floor.

"Eeeewww! Gross," Irma said as she watched the critter go. "Now it's *really* giving me the creeps!"

"I can't believe it," Will said. "That ray from the Heart must have shrunk it."

Taranee's mouth went dry for a moment as she contemplated the Guardians' power.

Clank! Clank! Clankclankclank!

Taranee started. She gazed down the corridor in amazement. One by one, the bars of the tiny prison cells were bursting open!

Turning to Will, she announced, "The Heart did a lot more than take care of that beastly insect. I don't know how, but it opened up all of the cells!"

Once again, Taranee thought with a sigh, our magic has unleashed more than we bargained for. Let the chaos begin!

TWELVE

Elyon paced. She was doubting her brother's promise, doubting his assurance that her parents would be protected. In short, she was doubting everything.

Finally, Elyon couldn't take it anymore. She needed to check on her parents. She would get to the prison, she decided, on foot.

Hidden beneath her hooded brown cloak, she left the palace and began walking through the kingdom she was destined to rule. As she glided, undetected, through the gray streets, she was struck by the people's despair. Green-and-blue children were subdued as they played their ragtag street games. Merchants counted their scanty coins and scowled. Mothers clutched baskets of hard bread and dried-up vegetables and hurried home without stopping to chat with friends.

When I am queen, Elyon thought pensively, maybe things will be different. Maybe I could use part of Phobos's garden to grow better food. I could let people into the palace. I don't know why Phobos shuts everyone out, anyway. It's so cold and lonely there!

Elyon's trudging steps grew lighter as she neared the trail that led to the brooding, mountaintop prison. It was just beginning to dawn on her that maybe *she* could help make things better in Metamoor. A title like Light of Meridian certainly boded well, didn't it? Maybe that sunny picture she'd drawn as a little girl *could* become a reality.

Hope filled Elyon's body, warming her. At the same time, she felt a sense of excitement building around her. Nearby, a long-eared Metamoorian grabbed another by the shoulders and breathlessly announced something.

Other townspeople began talking animatedly. They glanced toward the prison with wide eyes.

It's a good thing I left the palace, Elyon thought. Something very strange is happening.

Elyon stepped closer to two chattering Metamoorians to try to eavesdrop on their conversation.

"Hurry up, Halgart!" one said to the other. "Call the others. Call everyone!"

A female creature behind Elyon grabbed her bedraggled little boy and began to push him through the curtained doorway of a small shop.

"Get the little ones inside," she cried. "It's an uprising! The prison's been opened!"

From under the cover of her heavy hood, Elyon gasped. She began to hurry toward the prison. A throng of Metamoorians had begun to gather at the base of the hill below the prison. Soldiers were assembling, too, wielding axes, sabers, and spears. But the people's exuberance wasn't squelched. They were laughing and shouting and . . .

. . . Carrying my friends on their shoulders? Elyon suddenly realized in amazement.

It was true! Off in the distance, hoisted high above the crowd, Elyon could see Will, Irma, Hay Lin, Taranee, and Cornelia. They were in their glam Guardian forms. Irma was pumping her fist in triumph. Taranee was glowing with pride. And Cornelia? She was scanning the crowd with searching eyes.

She's looking for me, Elyon thought. She took a halting step closer to the crowd. She was getting ready to call out to her friends when she saw two other people she knew.

They were Metamoorians, but they weren't jumping around like their compatriots. They weren't laughing or singing, either. The woman's green face was pale and drawn. As she limped along, a man with mossy dread-locks and worried purple eyes supported her with both hands.

It's my parents! Elyon thought. But my mother's hurt. What have they done to her?

Elyon took another step forward. This time, her path was blocked by a giant guard cracking a whip in the air. The creature glared down at a cowering green teenager. The youth wore a brown cloak just like Elyon's.

"This area is off-limits," he growled. "Move away, peasant!"

"But my brother is down there," the thin young man protested. "Don't you believe me?"

"Oh, I believe you," the soldier grunted. He raised his whip high over his head again. "The prison is the only place for dogs like you."

Shatzzzz!

The soldier brought the whip down on the boy's back, sending the skinny Metamoorian sprawling.

"No!" Elyon screamed. The word burst from her mouth before she could stop herself.

The soldier glared threateningly at her. Elyon's first instinct was to duck back beneath her hood and slither away. Then she realized something.

I don't need to stop myself from speaking out, she thought. I don't want—*I won't have*—this kind of oppression in my city!

"No!" she shouted again. This time, she raised her arm in the air as she issued the order. An invisible bolt of magic shot from her hand, knocking the whip right out of the soldier's claw.

"What the—?" he blurted out.

Elyon clenched her fists. She felt her pale cheeks flush with anger. The rage quickly turned to magic, which burst from her body in sparkling, white rays. Her power destroyed her brown cloak. Underneath her rags, Elyon wore an ice-blue dress—the garment of a queen.

"That horrible prison," she roared, "is good for nobody! It's a mistake. A huge mistake!"

Remember, Elyon. You can erase any mistake.

Elyon paused. A voice made of memories had suddenly flooded her mind. It was her mother's! Elyon remembered her mother handing her that little, pink eraser. Her shock, desperation, and outrage melted away as she remembered the simple motion that had, long ago, erased the mistake from her drawing.

Any mistake . . . Elyon thought now. Any mistake at all.

Looking up, she passed her hand before her face, blocking the sight of the ugly, hilltop prison. When her eyes refocused, the prison had become enveloped in a blanket of white light.

In a cloak of magic.

By Elyon's own mystical eraser.

A moment later, the entire prison of Meridian disappeared!

All around her, Elyon was dimly aware of Metamoorians, crying out in shock and shouting out the news, although all of those in Meridian could see it for themselves.

Elyon herself, however, was calm.

I've erased the mistake, she thought. I did it for the woman whom, deep in my heart, I still consider to be my mother. And for the citizens of Meridian . . . my own people.

The remedy had taken but an instant. It had been so swift that nobody could believe their eyes.

Not the Guardians of the Veil, who gazed at the mountaintop in awe.

Not the milling Metamoorians, who'd been haunted by that prison for generations.

And not Eleanor Brown.

Eleanor wasn't looking at the now-barren hilltop. Instead, she was searching through the crowd for the little blond girl who would one day be queen.

"Elyon?" she called.

Her mother's voice was soft, and yet Elyon could hear it over the clamor of the crowd. When she saw her, she let out a silent sob. At that moment, she didn't feel like a queen-to-be. She felt like a little girl torn from her home, confused, terrified, longing for the embrace she used to know so well.

"Mom?" she called back.

All Elyon wanted was to rush to her mother, to be her daughter once again. But someone in the crowd had spotted her. He was crying out,

"It's her! Elyon! The Light of Meridian!"

Immediately, Elyon was surrounded by adoring Metamoorians. They took her hands in their gentle claws and grinned into her stunned face. They knelt at her feet in gratitude. Her ears began to ring with exclamations of praise.

"Did you see that?" one man yelled triumphantly. "She destroyed the prison!"

"She's come for us!" another cried gratefully.

"Long live the Light of Meridian!" shouted a woman nearby.

Now it was Elyon who was hoisted onto the shoulders of her people. At first, she tried to squirm out of their grasp. She didn't want to be celebrated. She wanted to be with her friends, the Guardians. She could see them now, slipping into the crowd. No doubt they were sneaking back to their portal, escaping Metamoor before Phobos could set his soldiers upon them.

Elyon looked from her friends' retreating backs to her parents. They, too, were stealing toward the edge of the crowd. Vathek was waiting for them there. He was going to take Thomas and Eleanor to a hiding place. Elyon felt relief flood through every part of her body.

Elyon's mother had perked up, too. She was no longer limping. She had strength enough to glance back at Elyon with a teary-eyed smile.

Elyon met her mother's eyes.

Maybe, she thought as the celebratory crowd bore her away, Elyon and the Light of Meridian aren't so far apart after all. I may be a queen, but I'm also a daughter. Thomas and Eleanor Brown are my parents—I don't care what anybody else says.

Elyon took one last glimpse at her mother. She wished she could tell her how she felt.

Her mother nodded back at her and smiled more broadly.

Somehow, Elyon thought happily, I think she knows. Of course she does. She's my mom.

With that knowledge, Elyon felt free finally to turn away, to accept the gratitude of her people, and to celebrate with them.

It looks as if light, Elyon thought triumphantly, is dawning in Meridian!

THIS WAY, MCTIENNANI! I KNOW I SAW A LIGHT COMING FROM THE BASEMENT.

THAT'S STRANGE. THE ELECTRICITY'S OUT.

HI! WHAT BRINGS YOU FOLKS HERE?

WE THOUGHT YOU MIGHT BE HERE.

BUT WE COULD ASK YOU THE SAME QUESTION.

LATER ON, IN FRONT OF CORNELIA'S HOUSE . . .

THANKS FOR GOING WITH ME, WILL. THANKS FOR EVERYTHING!

NO PROBLEM! THE IMPORTANT THING IS THAT WE SHOOK OFF THOSE AGENTS.

DO YOU THINK THEY BOUGHT THE STORY ABOUT HAVING A GET-TOGETHER IN MEMORY OF ELYON AT HER HOUSE?

I DOUBT IT. BUT I COULDN'T COME UP WITH ANYTHING BETTER . . .

". . . AND AGENT MEDINA REALLY SHOWED US HOW TOUGH SHE WAS."

LET'S JUST GO! WE HAVE NO REASON TO KEEP THE GIRLS ANY LONGER.

I'M TELLING YOU, THERE WAS A GIANT IN THE BACK OF THIS VAN. A REAL MONSTER AND . . .

YEAH, YOU'RE RIGHT! THAT'S ONE GIANT. . . DOG!

WOOF WOOF